Transatlantic Ticket 1852

Passage to the New World

BY JAN FRAZIER

Hellgate Press   Ashland, OR

Transatlantic Ticket 1852
©2018 Janice Frazier

Published by Hellgate Press
(An imprint of L&R Publishing, LLC)

Hellgate Press
PO Box 3531
Ashland, OR 97520
email: sales@hellgatepress.com

Interior design: Sasha Kincaid
Cover design: L. Redding

Library of Congress Cataloging-in-Publication Data available from the publisher on request.

ISBN: 978-155571-893-0

Printed and bound in the United States of America
10 9 8 7 6 5 4 3 2 1

This book is dedicated to the many German emigrants that braved the Atlantic Ocean in pursuit of freedom and a new life in America. Especially, it is dedicated to my great-grandparents, Christian and Elizabeth Haas Pollmann and their families, who came to Illinois in search of religious freedom, employment opportunities, and a new beginning of life.

Table of Contents

VI TRANSATLANTIC TICKET 1852

Acknowledgments

I want to thank my Pollmann cousins – Edith, Peter, Ruben, and Felix – in Hummersen, Germany, for all of the information that they provided to me concerning Lipperland and for the valuable time that they spent with me during my many visits to their home.

Also, I want to acknowledge and thank the volunteers at the Tazewell County Historical and Genealogical Society for the hours that they spent in helping me research my Pollmann ancestors.

In addition, I want to acknowledge and thank Shane Grimes – a senior at Bradley University, Peoria, IL – for the amazing book cover. Shane has an incredible talent, and I'm so grateful to him for all of his work. Thank you, Shane!

Introduction

The book is a compilation of fact and fiction. Elizabeth and Christian Pollmann were actual people — my great-grandparents. Christian was born in 1826 in the tiny village of Hummersen, Germany. My great-grandmother, Elizabeth Haas, was born in 1837 in Hergershausen, Germany. In reality, they were married in Pekin, Illinois, but to create a more realistic, intriguing story, the reading audience sees Christian and Elizabeth as being wed in Hummersen and already having two children when they sailed on the *Don Quixote* to New York City.

Christian arrived on May 6, 1852. He had a brother, Fredrich Pollmann already in America, making the transition in America far more viable for Chris. In actuality, Elizabeth arrived *alone* in America on the *Saxonia* on October 8, 1862. Elizabeth's mother was Anna Margaretha Weber and her father was Johann Adam Haas. Her maternal grandmother was Elizabeth Reuling, and with the many Reulings living in the Pekin area, I have to believe that she had some relatives in the city to help her adjust to the New World.

Having first visited Hummersen during the summer of 2006, I had the privilege of meeting Pollmanns still living in that incredibly beautiful community called Lipperland. It was amazing to see the Falkenhagen Church where my great-grandfather, Christian, was baptized and confirmed. I walked the small well-worn path, leading around the church, that people in the 1800s as well as today tread to get to the large, wooden doors that open to the remarkably splendid yet simple sanctuary. With tear-filled eyes, I stood in the tiny room used by the confirmands. There, my great-grandfather had sat learning the word of God as dictated in the mid-nineteenth century. In Schwalenburg, I saw the magnificently gilded Town Hall where Christian Pollmann walked in order to get his papers to come to the New World. And last of all, I visited the Pollmann homestead — still inhabited by Pollmanns — where he was born and lived until he left for Illinois.

The visit to Hummersen was an amazing experience that I'll never forget. I've visited many times since that first incredible visit, and my thanks to my cousins, Edith, Peter, Ruben, and Felix Eichleiter for an awesome trip "back in time" into the village and life-style of Hummersen, Germany.

In addition, I found the other side of my German family in Wilgartswiesen some years later, and if you enjoy this book, you might like *Prairie Points - A Civil War Sanctuary,* which is about the Dully family as they arrive in the New World. Also, *European Roots and Beyond* tells of the funny experiences I had with both sides of my family as I tried to discover who they were and where they lived. Since first going to meet the Eichleiters in Hummersen and then the Dullys in Wilgartswiesen, we have had countless reunions both in Germany and in America. It has been an incredible experience for everyone.

I want to add that this was one of the easiest books for me to write. I felt as if my great-grandfather were sitting on my shoulder guiding my mind and hand. I did a great deal of research for this book; however, much of it seemed to be "spoken" to me in my mind by an all-knowing voice, which I believe was my great-grandfather, Christian Pollmann. It was actually eerie. Also, this is the second publication of this book as I wanted to add pictures to enhance the story.

Here's hoping that you enjoy *Transatlantic Ticket 1852.*

One

LIFE IN GERMANY – 1852

A slice of golden moon showed in the midnight sky, which was filled with dusky starlight. It was Germany, 1852, and Christian Pollmann — still fully clothed — sat on his front porch in the village of Hummersen. The February air was brisk as a chill made him pull his worn jacket closer around his body. Chris focused on the splendor of the North Star and wondered how an awesome sky so full of beauty could shine brilliance on a world filled with chaos and uncertainty.

With an unstable political situation in 1848, revolutionary acts broke out in opposition to authoritarian governments. However, as the Revolution failed, the existing monarch placed even stricter regulations upon the common Germany people, causing many families to focus their hopes and dreams on the New World, America. Such were Christian's thoughts as he sat alone, engulfed by the black night; a feeling of hopelessness surrounded him which was lessened only by letters from his brother in Illinois who gave him hope for a new life abroad.

"Chris?" The voice came from the inside of the house where Christian saw a candle burning at the door.

"Chris, what's wrong? What are you doing out there?" Even though the voice was quiet, there was strength and endurance in its tone.

"Thinking, Elizabeth. Just thinking."

"It's cold and late. Come inside to think," his young wife begged.

Slowly, Chris got up from the old wooden chair. He was a tall, lanky man, mid-twenties. His blonde hair and blue eyes were indicative of the "master race" that in less than a hundred years would become a symbol for Hitler's regime.

The door was opened by a slight figure of a woman, beautiful nonetheless as the candlelight played upon her long brown hair, brown eyes, and olive complexion. With Italian ancestors on her mother's side of the family, she didn't meet the qualifications of a pure German woman — not in physical features, anyway — but she had the mental strength of the German Frau and the fortitude needed to work long, hard hours in the house as well as in the field if necessary.

"Chris," Elizabeth commented as she stoked the fire, whose embers were still red, "What's wrong? You've not been yourself in days. When I talk to you, you're only listening with one ear."

Chris had hung his jacket on a hook near the door and now stood looking out the curtained window. Even though there wasn't extra money, Elizabeth insisted on nice curtains on the windows and a rug before the fireplace.

"Chris?"

"Yeah, what is it, Elizabeth?"

"You haven't heard a word I've said, have you?"

"You asked me what I was doing outside."

"No, I asked you what was wrong. You're not yourself. I share everything with you — every personal problem that I have. What are you keeping from me, dear husband?"

Christian moved slowly towards the fire, accepting the cup of coffee she offered him. Elizabeth always kept soup and coffee warm at the fireplace — one more thing she felt important in her household. Even though Elizabeth had a second-hand iron cook stove in the kitchen, she still preferred the fireplace. She had learned to cook and bake on the fire, and it brought back precious memories of her earlier years.

"Okay, Elizabeth. Sit down, please."

Elizabeth got a cup of coffee for herself and took a seat on the bench across from her husband. He looked tired, she thought — not just exhausted from a long physical day but also from mental anguish. She waited.

Christian took a sip of the warm brew, looking into the cup as if it offered answers. "I'm worried about our future here," he finally commented.

"Here, in this house?" she questioned quietly.

"No, in this country, Elizabeth — in Germany."

Her heart sank at her husband's words. "It's Georg, isn't it? He's talking nonsense to you again. Why do you let him upset you?"

Christian's brother, Georg, three years his senior, often coerced Chris into doing things to which Elizabeth objected. He meddled in their business — both personal and financial — and Elizabeth often felt that her husband was undermined. Several ventures of selling crops to Georg's acquaintances in Hummersen had resulted in little or no profit, and Christian had learned that Georg had not always had his brother's best interest in mind.

"No, it's not Georg, Well, at least it's not him entirely," he added. "With the failed Revolution, Germany has changed for the worse. Taxes have increased drastically; the government continues with strict, unbelievable regulations; churches are being unified according to the government's wishes; and now the inheritance laws have changed so that only the oldest son will inherit anything."

The thoughts literally rolled off Chris' tongue as if he had struggled to contain them, and now they were finally being regurgitated with despondence. Sounding as if he had practiced this speech many times, Chris felt a bit embarrassed at the velocity of his words. The fact was, he had gone over everything in his mind hundreds of times, and it was truly a relief to let them out, and he breathed a long sigh of relief.

In softer tones, he concluded with downcast eyes, "We can barely clothe the children and now the potato blight has made the food supply short. You know this winter has been a nightmare."

"We've made it, though, Chris." Elizabeth tried to drive home a point, but it sounded feeble.

"Barely — we made it barely these past months. How about next winter? It's going to get worse, Elizabeth."

Elizabeth clung to the hope that they could raise enough crops for a profit so that they wouldn't be forced to move — away from her parents and younger sisters. She had hoped that maybe she could take in sewing and mending for the upper class, but with two children, there had been precious little time.

"Maybe you should try to get a job again as a cabinet maker," she suggested. "You did well after your apprenticeship. We shouldn't have let Georg talk you into farming part of your father's land."

"I was glad to help my father, but under the new inheritance laws, eventually, all of this land will go to the eldest — Georg — and we'll have nothing. I think cabinet making is what I need to do again, but not here," Christian concluded.

Elizabeth's eyes met her husband's. A tightening in her stomach kept her from asking the inevitable — how far would he want to move? Bavaria? To a big city — Munich or even Berlin? Finally, Elizabeth choked the word, "Where?"

Christian didn't answer. Silently, he placed his cup on the nearby table and covered his face with hands for a moment. Eventually, he found the courage to look at Elizabeth's wide-eyed stare as he whispered, "Away from our fatherland of Germany. America, Elizabeth, America."

* * * *

Chris watched Elizabeth's olive skin pale at the word "America." Looking down at her coffee, her hand shook slightly as she sat the cup on the bench. Not looking at her husband, she folded her hands as she felt a tear trickle down her cheek.

Finally, she found the strength to utter, "It's so far. We'd never see our families again." Her dark eyes — now wet with tears — finally rose to meet her husband's. His strong, solemn face and firm-set eyes usually gave her strength but not tonight.

"You and the children are my family. You promised to leave your mother and father and forsake all others for me. What was that, five year ago? Remember, Elizabeth?"

Silently, she nodded.

"My brother Fredrich has been in America for almost two years. He has earned enough money for his wife Louisa and the three children to join him now in Illinois. We could go with them. There's work, food, and hope, Elizabeth. It's not a land for the weak of spirit or for men who can't work long, hard hours. Fredrich says that he never knew real work ethics until he went to America. The pioneers there work with perseverance and efficiency unknown in Germany. But the hard work pays off. He already owns a small plot of land and raises his own food and also works as a carpenter. When his children arrive, they will be well fed and will go to school — a public school."

Chris paused, waiting for a response. There was none.

"Elizabeth, I want Margaretha and Anna-Marie to have a better life than this. The rich are getting richer here, the poor poorer. For the children to go to school means that I need more money, and we're not among the rich. The Revolution of 1848 failed. Heinrich von Gagern had such an ambitious plan to create a modern, liberal constitution for a unified Germany. Unfortunately, the National Assembly at St. Paul's Church led by von Gagern failed because of the many setbacks. Now, we live in a Germany that I don't know.

"It was bad before 1848 but impossible today. Basically, the feudal, militaristic systems are being re-established. As you know, General von Wrangel has already led troops through Frankfurt, re-capturing the city with his troops, who have earned the nickname 'street sweepers.' I understand that they yield only to violence. Otto von Bismarck and Fredrich Wilhelm are also gaining old power. Who knows what all of them will do to us."

Again, Christian paused. "Our neighbors are gone, Elizabeth. The Meiers left for American last year, and the Dulleys and Zimmermans left in 1848, along with hundreds of other German families throughout the country. Actually, the Dulleys live close to Fredrich."

Elizabeth spoke for the first time since the start of the conversation. "The Dulleys aren't close, Chris. They're hundreds of kilometers apart."

"Well, they are in Indiana, and Fredrich lives in Illinois. I think that's pretty close considering the size of America." He shrugged and smiled as Elizabeth mustered a grin.

"Christian," Elizabeth whispered as she, too, sensed that they belonged to a life that was gone, and she wiped a final tear from her cheek. "This conversation isn't a total shock to me. I saw the stars in your eyes when our neighbors left us and went to the New World. I've watched you daydream quietly for over a year and was sure you were thinking of this. I couldn't ask, though, for fear I was right. But I knew when I married you that you wouldn't settle for a poor life. In fact, your drive and ambition are what attracted me to you — always striving to be better, wanting more, and expecting the best." Elizabeth paused as she reached for Christian's hand. "You never have to convince me of your plans. The children and I go wherever you go and whenever you are ready."

Christian pulled his wife towards him, folding his arms around her body. "We'll have a new life, my love. I can feel it. Wait to tell the children and our parents, though. Let's get arrangements in place first."

Elizabeth nodded. Chris felt his wife's body stiffen slightly as she pulled away.

"What is it?" he asked, watching a worried look continue to darken his wife's face. Only once before had he seen this same distressed look, and that was when he had told her that they were leaving their cozy home in the village for a small farmhouse in rural Hummersen.

"Chris, I'm frightened." Elizabeth felt her stomach tighten again as she looked into her husband's eyes. "I'm very frightened."

"Me, too, but we can do this," he answered as he placed his arms once again around her. "We'll talk tomorrow. It's late." He kissed her lightly on the lips, hoping that he saw a glimmer of hope in her eyes as he got up to ready himself for bed.

As he walked past the window, Chris noticed that the brilliance of the night was now slightly hidden by clouds, which rolled in from the east. He stood looking at the changing atmosphere of the midnight sky with his eyes still focused on the unchanging North Star.

"God help us through this difficult life," he whispered, "whether we're in Germany or America. Life is a struggle, but it's all for you, Lord." Christian's religious strength had come from his Lutheran mother — who eventually joined the Evangelical Church — and he leaned on her foundation continually as life seemed impossible to bear at times. However, now it seemed more difficult.

The stars — including the North Star — were nearly completely hidden now as a clap of thunder was followed by the rain pelting against the window.

"Winter storm coming?" Elizabeth asked, picking up the two coffee cups now empty and carrying them to the dry sink in the kitchen.

Christian hoped that he was hearing the old lilt in his wife's voice — that optimistic tone, which had carried them through many difficult times.

"Yeah, I think so."

Christian's thoughts again returned to the storm that had been brewing in Germany for years now, knowing that it was his sole wish to escape. However, what he didn't anticipate was that the storms were fierce not only on the continent of Europe but also on the open waters of the Atlantic and on the vast prairie lands of America. What he didn't know was that he and his family would never escape the storms wherever they went. However, Christian — optimistic as he was — would always possess faith and hope in his family's future.

Two

THE WILD MIDWEST

The sun was still below the horizon when Elizabeth awoke to a new day. As she rolled over to get up, her feet felt the cold floor, and she scurried into her underclothes and worn dress. She had not slept well — her thoughts and dreams had been twisted with nightmarish premonitions of the future. As she sat to pull on her woolen stockings, she felt an overwhelming wave of melancholy. America — she had heard stories. There was freedom of speech and religion, but there were also frightening stories of the wild frontier.

Elizabeth's best friend, Wilhelmina, had a sister who had gone to America. Dorthea had left three years ago with her husband, Peter, and three children. Landing in New York, they took a train to Missouri where Peter's uncle had a farm. Staying with the uncle and his family worked temporarily until Dorthea and Peter had enough money to buy a few acres of land and build a log cabin. By the second year, twins were born and another room was added to the cabin.

Dorthea's letters were always upbeat — the day's work was long, hard, and sometimes grueling, but the rewards were overwhelming. They had ample food, freedom to worship, and a government with representation of the people. Dorthea urged her sister to join them in America. Wilhelmina was actually considering the possibilities. Because she was unmarried and working at Frohmeir's Tailor Shop in Hummersen, she thought the idea of America sounded exciting and offered her a new future.

Then the letters from Dorthea ceased for six months. At first, Wilhelmina thought that the spring weather and work in the fields were occupying Dorthea's time. However, as the summer waned, Wilhelmina became anxious and tried to reach Peter's uncle by mail.

One cold evening in October, a knock sounded on the door of Wilhelmina's room that she rented above the general store. No one called on her after dark, and Wilhelmina was hesitant. Calling out to the visitor, she couldn't understand what was being said, but she thought she recognized the voice. It was a familiar voice but whose? Listening again, she stood frozen — Peter. Flinging open the door, she found a ragged, thin skeleton of a man, barely recognizable. Although his eyes were sunken and dull, they were Peter's.

Stumbling in, Peter made his way to a chair and slumped his tired body down with a long, heavy sigh. Already crying, Wilhelmina anticipated the worst. Slowly, Peter stammered through the story.

It had been May, and he had been in the field late that night. With extra funds from the harvest, they had bought twenty more acres, and Peter had been in a far field planting corn. It was 10 o'clock when he reached the house, and immediately he knew something was awry. No candles glowed in the windows, and no smoke curled from the chimney.

Sometime during the day, a small but wild band of Indians had come through the area and raided all unsuspecting houses. They were Comanches and had made their way to Missouri from Oklahoma, randomly striking villages and slaughtering their victims. Frantically, word was spread of the Indians, but not all households received the message, and, unfortunately, Dorthea was one of them.

Now crying uncontrollably, Wilhelmina was unable to listen to what Peter found that night in the little log cabin. People in the 1800s were used to deaths — they were frequent and often occurred to babies and children due to illness. But Wilhelmina could not accept this — it was insane, savage murder.

Peter had lost his senses for several days. When the neighbors found him sitting in the cabin, he — as well as the rooms — was drenched in blood. His neighbor said that as he sat in a rocking chair, Peter's eyes were glazed over as he held one of his daughter's dolls, rocking and singing it to sleep.

For the next three months, Peter searched for that band of Comanches. Not caring if he lived or died, he carried his rifle as he rode from town to town, going into Illinois and Indiana. Some villages had seen the Indians weeks before, but Peter never got close to them, and, finally, losing all hope, he returned to Missouri. By September he wanted nothing but to return to Germany.

During the weeks that followed, Wilhelmina tried to nurse him back to health, but mentally she couldn't help Peter. Nightmares plagued him at night, and visions of Dorthea and the children haunted him all day. Eventually, Peter was declared insane and put into an asylum.

This story flashed through Elizabeth's mind for the um-teenth time since last night when Chris had first mentioned America. Was this incident a fluke or did it happen often to people living in the wilderness of the Midwest? Even though most stories she had heard were positive, the tragic ones were cemented into her mind.

As Elizabeth lit a candle and tiptoed to the door, her glance fell on Christian's side of the bed, which was empty. Opening the bedroom door to the already warm living room, Elizabeth knew that her husband had stoked the fire hours earlier. Sitting in the rocking chair, he was staring at the flames, his hands folded in his lap.

"Chris?"

He turned, revealing tired eyes that hadn't closed that night.

"Are you okay, Christian?"

He nodded.

"You're thinking about America?" Elizabeth asked.

"Yes, it's just that all of this seemed so simple and right in my daydreams. Now that I've told you, I'm worried that it's not best for you and the children."

Elizabeth wanted to blurt out the story that had been haunting her, but instead she went to her husband and placed her arms around his neck.

"Whatever is best for you is right for us, too, my love. Now, a decision has been made, and there's lots of planning to do. You can't do that if you haven't slept."

His grin was full of relief as he rose to kiss Elizabeth's cheek. Was the darkness truly gone from her face or did he just imagine it?

"Thank you, Elizabeth. I needed to hear that from you. Although you said it last night, I needed reassurance."

"Now, you go and get an hour's sleep," Elizabeth smiled, brushing his hair from his eyes. "I'll do the morning chores. Scoot now," she said, shooing him away as she would a child.

Christian quickly and quietly crossed the room, closing the bedroom door behind him. As Elizabeth turned her attention to readying the kitchen and the fire for breakfast, she looked around the combined living room-dining room area. Thinking this would always be home, the two had considered adding a loft as the family grew. They had already added a front porch the previous year and an enlarged vegetable garden in back. Elizabeth covered her eyes with her hands as if to block the disturbing thoughts from her mind.

However, Elizabeth knew that these new plans — frightening as they were — must not deter her or her family, and she attempted to shake off the dismal thoughts clouding her mind. Always an optimistic person, she decided that — as always — she must trust God with their future. At this moment, she again vowed that she and Chris would take each step one at a time, conquering all the struggles and tribulations that occurred. Silently, she thanked her parents for raising her and her sisters with strong wills and deep religious beliefs. Strong Protestants in a world of Catholicism sometimes had their difficulties, but Elizabeth's parents taught her to uphold her theological beliefs.

As she went to the window to open the curtains, she twinged, thinking about having to tell her family and then realized that they, too, could handle this situation because of their inner strength. The sun's rays were just beginning to glow orange on the horizon, promising a beautiful day, and Elizabeth seized onto the thought that America, too, would have the same sunrises and the same beautiful days.

Three

HEINRICH POLLMANN

Christian didn't bother to change into nightclothes, but quickly slipped out of his heavy boots and slid under the warm down comforter. He barely hit the bed when he fell into a deep sleep, and for three hours, he was dead to the world. Not having slept well for several nights and struggling with uncertainty about Elizabeth's reaction concerning America, Chris now relaxed, feeling that Elizabeth was in favor of the difficult decision that he had mentally made weeks before. Hours later and deep into a dream, Chris felt as if he were rocking on a boat as he awoke to Elizabeth shaking him.

"Christian, I hate to wake you, but your father is here."

"What time is it?" Chris asked as he quickly swung his legs out of bed. "I feel as if I've slept for days."

"It's mid-morning. Chores are done, and I just took bread from the oven so it's fresh for you and your father."

Pulling on his boots, Elizabeth handed him a clean shirt as he took off the one he was still wearing from the day before.

"Does my father know that I was in bed?"

"No, he just knows that you're in the bedroom," Elizabeth answered.

Christian opened the door to find his father standing near the window, looking out at the rows of unplowed fields that stretched north from the house. A cold drizzle mixed with snow had started. The morning sun was obscured by the heavy clouds, and it looked as if the day would be dark and dreary.

Margaretha — who was now four — and three-year-old Anna-Marie were sitting by the open fire, entranced with dressing their dolls. Elizabeth had made each girl a rag doll for Christmas along with two dresses a piece, and the children daily entertained themselves for hours as they bathed, dressed, fed, and rocked their babies.

"Opa, come look at Emma. She has just had her bath," Margaretha called. Heinrich Pollmann caught sight of his son entering the room as he turned towards his granddaughter.

"Margaretha, she looks beautiful — clean and happy," Heinrich smiled as he walked over to pat his granddaughter's head, hanging full with long, beautiful curls. Margaretha was tiny with her mother's olive complexion and dark hair. Anna-Marie resembled the Pollmanns — fair with blue eyes. She had a bigger body structure, making her already as tall as her older sister.

"Good morning, Christian. Are you well?"

Chris resembled his father who was also tall, lanky, and blonde, but graying at the temples. Although still a handsome man, Heinrich was showing age lines in his face and a slightly bent stature indicated his over-fifty years.

"Yes, I'm fine. I was changing my shirt." He hoped his father wouldn't ask further questions, not knowing how he would explain sleeping at this hour of the day. Quickly, he added, "Please, sit down, Pa. Elizabeth has just baked bread."

Already she had sliced the warm loaf and was letting the creamery butter soak into the thick slices when Christian pulled up chairs at the table for his father and him.

Over a cup of coffee drowned in rich cream and sugar plus several slices of Elizabeth's delicious bread, the men talked of the upcoming planting season and problems already sprouting with an abundance of rain and unseasonably cold weather. Last year's crops had been sparse with a too-cool summer — not enough sun plus excessive moisture. The potato blight had now reached

Germany and other parts of Europe after its beginnings in Ireland, and farmers had suffered from all-around poor harvests of their crops.

As the conversation seemed to wane, Heinrich took a letter from his pocket and dropped it onto the table. Immediately, Chris knew it was from Fredrich, and he quickly glanced at Elizabeth who was bringing them fresh coffee. Avoiding Christian's eyes and pretending not to see the letter, she poured coffee into their cups and returned to the kitchen.

"Fredrich has sent for Louisa and the children," Heinrich remarked.

"Yes, I know. I went to check on Louisa several days ago, and she told me." Chris paused, trying to cover his own feelings of excitement and asked, "What do you think about them going?"

"I hate to see them leave because I'll probably never see them again. It was very difficult on your mother to see Fredrich go, and she has known that it was only a matter of time before Louisa and the three children would leave. However, Fredrich is doing well, and they all will have a promising future in America. There's nothing for us in Germany — no future for any of us, especially young people with families. If only we had fought harder — and longer — in the Revolution, things might be different now."

Heinrich had been active in the Marzrevolution (March Revolution of 1848). When crops failed in the fall of 1847, hunger riots led by desperate workers — including Heinrich — were suppressed by the German militia. By March, 1848, Germany was a tinderbox, waiting for a spark to ignite its contents. When King Fredrich Wilhelm IV of Prussia declined to grant a constitution, public protests increased. On March 17, 1848, King Wilhelm finally yielded to almost all of the public demands, and a delighted crowd became a little too exuberant and tried to enter the palace. Shots that were fired into the crowd created a riot, and as fierce fighting erupted, 250 civilians were left dead. Heinrich was among that riotous group of civilians that March night and, thus, felt the results of the Revolution first hand.

"I'm worried about Louisa and the children going alone on the boat. There are many undesirable people on the ships plus fatal diseases. Cholera runs rampant on some of the ships with only half of the passengers arriving in America."

Christian glanced at Elizabeth who pretended not to hear.

"It's a long, arduous trip for a man, but for a woman with children, it's much worse." Heinrich paused for a moment, pondering. "But thousands have gone under worse conditions than Louisa. Last year, I heard of a lady in Detmold who took her seven children — two of whom were twins who were only seven months old — to meet her husband already in Pennsylvania. She went alone, caring for all of the children on the boat, and then when they got to America, they had to take two trains plus a horse-drawn buggy to get to their destination. An amazing feat," Heinrich said, shaking his head in admiration.

Christian was silent as he again lifted his eyes to look at Elizabeth. She was still in the kitchen in full view of the dining room, and she glanced up ever so quickly to catch his gaze. With the slightest motion, she nodded her head, and Chris — understanding her signal — turned to look directly at his father.

"Pa, I have something to tell you."

Christian wouldn't have had to say another word because his eyes told the entire story. There was hope and expectation shining in them, and Heinrich knew before Chris uttered another word that he had plans of going to the New World.

"Elizabeth, the girls, and I are going, too. I wanted to wait to tell you until everything was finalized, but the time seems right now."

"I'm not surprised, son. There's no hope here. Germany is going through a rough time, and there's no telling how long it'll last," he remarked with what Chris believed to be a pseudo-calm resolve. Knowing how close both Heinrich and Sophia had always been with their children, Chris knew that their move would be painful for his parents.

Elizabeth had moved over to put her hands on her father-in-law's shoulders. She glanced at the girls who remained engrossed in their play, unaware of the adult conversation. Already, she was feeling the pangs of separation from loved ones as she stood looking at Chris' father whom she adored. How would she react to telling her own parents and sisters? Brushing the thoughts aside, she took a seat between Heinrich and Chris.

"Will you go with Louisa?" Heinrich asked.

"That's what we hope."

"Christian, I can't say I want you to go. You know that. But it's good. You'll have a future in America." He was silent a moment. "Let's wait to tell your mother, though."

"Is she feeling better?" Christian asked.

In bed with a fever and relentless cough, Sophia Pollmann had been ill for several weeks. Christian's sister, Charlotte, had been nursing her back to health.

"She seems about the same, but she did sleep a little better last night. Charlotte actually rested some, too. Your sister has been at our house day and night these past two weeks. Katherine has been cooking and doing the washing while Charlotte waits on your mother."

Katherine and August, the youngest of the Pollmann children, were still at home while Charlotte, only recently married, had always been closest to her mother and quickly took it upon herself to return home when she heard of her mother's illness. Also blonde and blue-eyed, of the three girls, she was most like Christian, both physically and emotionally. Although Georg, Fredrich, and Christian were a tight-knit brotherly trio, his sister — little Charlotte — became someone truly special to Chris, winning his heart immediately. Calm and laid-back like Chris, the two siblings had been inseparable since she was born. Chris had been just over three years when Charlotte arrived, and he did what he could to help his mother. By the next year when Sophia was pregnant with Christina, Christian spent most of his time playing with his beloved younger sister.

"Yes, let's wait to tell her," Chris concluded. "It might be too upsetting."

As Heinrich rose to leave, he extended his hand to Chris and said one last time, "It's good, son. It's good."

"Opa, are you going?" Margaretha chimed in as Anna-Marie ran to him, rag doll flailing at her side. He scooped up his youngest granddaughter to plant a kiss on her cheek.

"I'll see you soon, girls. You two take care of your mother and father."

They giggled, and Margaretha scurried over to kiss her grandfather.

Heinrich gathered his coat and hat from the hook. The snow had stopped, and now a cold rain ceaselessly hit the window. Bundling up against the winter weather, Heinrich opened the door and bent against the blustery force of the icy rain. Definitely, another storm was brewing as the wind was now bending the ice-covered branches of the small oak tree nearly to the ground. Fog had gathered in the valley, and its cold, damp murkiness was an all-too-familiar sight. The deep winter months had been horrid because of food shortages from the previous fall harvests. Last year's cold, moist spring and summer had been plagued with foggy days and rainy nights, which alone would have created a sparse harvest. But the blight had only doubled the problems and so food bins remained nearly empty. Christian went to the door to suggest that his father wait until the weather cleared, but Heinrich waved the idea aside. Christian watched as his father unleashed his horse, Hannah, and climbed onto the wagon. With a quick wave to Chris and Elizabeth, he disappeared into the cloudy winter mist that seemed to envelope all of Germany.

Four

LOUISA RECEIVES THE NEWS

Within the next few days, Christian went to visit with Louisa. Living half a kilometer from Chris and Elizabeth, Louisa was just beyond the outskirts of Hummersen. Mary and Elise — age seven and six respectively — were hanging clothes on the line. It was a bright, clear February afternoon — with temperatures above 50 degrees — and all of the clotheslines in and around the village were full. Most of the days in the past few months had been drab and dull, so the afternoon sun was a godsend to chase away the wintry blues that seemed to encompass all of Hummersen. Young Karl — just turning four — was feeding the chickens when he saw Christian arrive.

"Uncle Chris," Karl yelled, dropping the bucket of food to the ground and running to greet his uncle.

Chris had other nieces and nephews — Georg had five children and Christina had two, but Karl was Chris' favorite. Quick to smile and laugh, little Karl seemed to have the natural ability to win people's hearts. Having lost two babies, both boys, Fredrich and Louisa felt blessed to have received this bundle of energy and love.

"I'm having a birthday in a few days," Karl chimed.

"How old are you going to be? Twenty?" Chris said with a grin.

Karl giggled as Christian stooped to receive a hug.

"Four, silly. I'll be four in two days."

"And you're the man of the house, right?"

"Yes, but we're going to America to be with Pa. He'll be man of the house again," Karl replied, his deep blue eyes sparkling.

"And you're excited?"

"Yes, I can't wait." Quickly, though, a look of sadness crossed his tiny face. "But that means I won't see you again, Uncle Chris." As fast as the melancholy expression appeared, it was replaced by a beaming smile as a new thought ran through the four-year-old's mind. "Maybe you can come to visit."

"I'm sure that can be arranged, Karl," Chris grinned, ruffling Karl's sandy blonde curls. "Where's your mother?"

"She's inside. I'll get her."

"No, I want to talk to her. I'll go in, but I'll see you again before I leave," Chris replied, sneaking a small piece of stick candy from his pocket and watching Karl's eyes light up. With his purchase of flour the previous day at Kiel's General Store, Gottlieb Kiel had given Chris one stick of candy to split between his girls. Chris had divided it into three parts so that he could give a piece to Karl.

Mary and Elise waved from the clothesline on the far side of the yard as Chris went to the front door, feeling a bit guilty that he didn't have more sweets to share. Already Louisa had heard Chris and Karl talking and had coffee brewing.

Louisa's long hours of work showed on her face as she had been both mother and father for almost two years. Just turning twenty-six in a few months, pre-mature gray flecked her long auburn hair, pulled back into a bun at the nape of her neck. Her usual lively blue eyes showed her weariness, but there was a glimmer, and she still possessed the same quick smile as Karl. Always a hard worker, Louisa had proved her stamina through the difficult autumn with a sparse harvest plus a bleak winter of little food and money. But now the long hours of 5:30 until 7:30 were taking their toll, and Louisa wanted nothing more than to be with her husband.

The two sat and discussed the weather, the children, Karl's upcoming birthday, and Sophia's illness before Christian broached the topic of going to America. Tears of happiness welled in Louisa's eyes as she received the news that Chris and Elizabeth were planning on selling their belongings and moving with her.

For months, she had been swept with grief and uncertainty as she faced the fear of a two-month dangerous voyage. Leaving her parents and siblings, plus being confronted with the prospect of an untamed frontier in America had increased her turbulent thoughts, and now she was overwhelmed with relief that she wouldn't be traveling alone. For half an hour, the two discussed future plans for the families, including selling belongings, purchasing tickets, and getting to Bremen to sail.

"It sounds as if Fredrich is doing well and likes the New World," Christian commented when there was a lull in the conversation.

"Yes. He has made enough money to purchase some acres to farm. The work is hard, but he seems to have only good things to say not only about America but also about the people. I think that he has met many friends through the church."

"I've noticed that the letters that I've read are full of news of the church. I'm not sure that he's totally behind all of the beliefs of the Lutheran Church in America, but he seems to enjoy the members of the congregation," Christopher concluded.

In 1817, King Fredrich Wilhelm III united the Lutheran Church of Germany with the Reformed Church, forming the Evangelical Church of Prussia. King Wilhelm had a personal reason for declaring the theological union. Because his wife was Lutheran and he was Reformed, they were unable to receive communion together; thus, the Evangelical Church seemingly solved that problem.

Originally strong Lutherans, the Pollmann family reluctantly had joined the Evangelical Church because there was no other option than to become Catholic — something unheard of for the Pollmanns. The Hohenzollern dynasty of King Fredrich Wilhelm III was not a union with which to reckon, and so the Pollmanns along with many other strong Lutherans felt persecuted.

Even in the early nineteenth century, hundreds of Prussian Protestants had sought total religious freedom by going to the New World. As the 1840s evolved and freedom of religion wasn't heightened, it also became one of Fredrich's primary reasons for leaving Germany.

"I, too, have had the feeling that Fredrich isn't totally behind the church's beliefs, but I still think he spends most of his spare time there. I would expect no less of him since church has always been a strong focus in his life," Louisa concluded.

And so it was with Christian — religion had been paramount as he grew up and as he chose a wife to bear his children. Since Christian's grandparents had resisted the ecumenical movement of the Evangelical Church in 1817, the Pollmann family had held firm to many of their Lutheran beliefs even though they attended the Evangelical Church after the 1817 reformation. Fredrich, however, was eventually finding that the Evangelical Church had had its effect on him and that he now held a mixture of beliefs — both Lutheran and Evangelical — and that the strong Lutheran Church in America was not totally to his liking.

"Louisa," Chris said as he continued to think of the voyage, "I've heard that adult prices have dropped to 100 Talers, and for children under twelve, it's 50 Talers. Under two, it's free. Right now I have money for four tickets."

"Prices have dropped?" Louisa questioned.

"Yes, I guess with more ships sailing, competition has picked up, and prices have gone down," Chris replied. "What about you — do you have enough money?"

"Yes, Fredrich sent more than enough," she replied.

"Good. And with selling our belongings, I hope to raise enough to get started in America. I hear the price of land is very cheap right now — around a dollar and a half an acre. I'm not sure what a Taler is worth in American dollars, but by selling our house, I should have enough money to get us to Illinois and perhaps buy a small farm sometime during the first year."

"Is any of the farm land in Hummersen yours?" Louisa asked.

"No, it's all Pa's. Georg will take over farming it." Chris paused, thinking. "Once in America, I may return to cabinet making as a second job if I can find time and have the energy," he smiled. "Many immigrants have two jobs, I understand."

For the past year, Christian had talked to every villager within miles who had a relative or friend in America. He listened and mentally tucked away all the necessary information he needed for success in the New World.

Louisa nodded. "Fredrich had two jobs at first, but now that he owns the farm, I think he has more than enough to do. Hopefully, I can ease the work load," she smiled, already anticipating the reunion with her husband. "By the way, we'll need to send what belongings we want to go to America two weeks before we sail."

"I had forgotten that — Fredrich sent a trunk, didn't he?"

Louisa nodded. "We can only take rucksacks on board," she added.

Already Louisa was mentally sifting through the children's belongings, knowing that many of their treasured articles would have to remain behind, replaced by bare necessities.

"Chris, have you told Elizabeth's parents?"

"No, only Pa knows. We're waiting to tell Ma when she gets stronger. Elizabeth will have to tell her folks when she feels the time is right."

Louisa and Christian discussed the prospect of getting their belongings sold by the end of March and making the trip together by train to Bremen. From there they would buy their tickets for passage and sail during the early spring, arriving in America in May with ample opportunity to become adjusted to the New World before winter set in. Now that she had family with whom to travel, Louisa felt renewed enthusiasm for leaving her fatherland for the strange wilderness known as Illinois.

As Chris bid Louisa and the children goodbye and left for home, it was late afternoon. The farmland along the way was barren. December and January had seen one heavy blizzard after another, and now February's days were a mixture of rain and snow, adding more moisture to the already over-saturated fields, and the skies continued to pour forth the wet, inclement weather. For a brief period that afternoon, the sun had broken through the clouds, and now its golden rays glowed on the western horizon. However brief, it was good to see color in the sky.

As Chris crested a peak of one of the mountains of Lipperland — the German name for Hummersen and its surrounding villages — he could now see his farmland stretched out in front of him. Only two years before, Chris remembered the acres of wheat, corn, and beans all basking in the warm spring and summer sun, which beamed down over the German hills and valleys. Northeastern Germany offered the perfect weather and growing season for a healthy harvest. Those days seemed to be over — at least temporarily.

His thoughts slowly drifted back to his childhood. Growing up, the Pollmanns' homestead was in the country. However, as Hummersen expanded, the rural area became urban, and Heinrich and Sophia now lived on the near outskirts of the town, with most of his farmland sold to the government for urban expansion. But back then, the lush green pasturelands of Lipperland were the playground for Christian and his siblings. With chores completed, the Pollmann children headed for the hills, covered with foot-high grasses, and played hide and seek until the sun started to fall below the horizon.

Always together, Chris and Charlotte used to sit down in the thick pasture and hide in the tall grasses for hours. The two never lacked for conversation as they sat hidden from the world. With the bond formed early in childhood, the two Pollmann children discussed every problem — not only childish traumas but also hopes and dreams for their futures.

Often last to meander home, Chris and Charlotte were at first punished for being late. However, Heinrich and Sophia eventually learned not to worry about them because they seemed to always take care of each other. Seemingly different from the rest, they were more level-headed as well as sensitive. They seemed to have been "cut from a different mold" than their siblings. All the Pollmann children upheld their responsibilities, but as youngsters, they wanted to run and play when chores were done. Chris and Charlotte, however, usually talked, dreamed, sang, and invented imaginary friends as they sat in the corner of the room as the others found mischief in the outdoors.

"They are our quiet ones, Heinrich," Sophia would often say to her husband who would worry that they were unlike the other children. "They're going to be philosophers," she'd state with a smile.

Being drawn from his reverie, Chris surveyed the land. As the economy changed, it seemed that the weather and the land followed suit. Devastation seemed to plague Chris' beloved Germany, and sadly he realized that he'd be leaving all of this behind. His children wouldn't grow up knowing the same joys he had experienced during his own childhood. They would come to know America — a foreign country — as their homeland.

A pang of melancholy swept over Christian as his eyes focused on his house in the distance. A wagon sat in front, tied to the picket fence. Company? At this time of day? He clicked the reins as the wagon wheels splashed over the muddy path leading to the Pollmann home. His stomach tightened as he wondered what visitors were calling so late.

Five

REGINA AND CONRAD MAKE PLANS

Kneading bread, Elizabeth sat by the open fire after Christian left. As she sat looking at the colorful sparks dancing from the logs, already she was feeling pains of sorrow tugging at her heart — leaving her family would be difficult. However, she knew that her husband was right — life as they had known it in Germany was over.

Elizabeth's father, Johann Haas, had been nearly as involved in the Revolution as Heinrich Pollmann. He had rallied along with other Germans to incite the leaders of the Revolution at the Frankfurt Parliament to use violence rather than intellectual debate against the government. The commoners were concerned that the Parliament had no military backing and that Heinrich von Gagern was too weak to be a leader and represent the general public.

And then in 1849 during the early post-revolutionary days, a delegation of the Frankfurt Parliament met with King Fredrich Wilhelm IV in Berlin, offering him the crown of Germany under the new constitution. He turned it down, saying he would not accept the offer because it came from revolutionaries — "from the gutter," he said. This was the final blow, and Johann Haas — along with his friends — also talked about leaving for the America. However, Elizabeth's mother, Anna, clung to her homeland, hoping that everything would eventually blow over and life in Germany would return to normal. What would she think now, Elizabeth wondered, when she got the news of hers and Christian's decision?

The sound of a wagon startled Elizabeth as she pulled herself from the reverie, and covering the kneaded loaf of bread with a moist cloth, she hurried towards the window. Already she heard the girls, who were playing on the porch, emit peals of laughter, and she knew that someone special was arriving.

From the window, she saw one of her younger sisters, Regina, step down from the wagon. Her husband, Conrad Kruse, was helping her as she struggled with her six-month bundle, Maria. The boys, Christoph and Gustav, were already running to play with their two cousins.

Elizabeth had a pot of pea soup cooking, and as the four children played, the grown-ups conversed. Regina — two years younger than Elizabeth — had her father's blonde curls and tall stature. Her pale, flawless complexion was duplicated in little Maria who looked like a china doll. Not having seen each other for several weeks, the sisters caught up on news as Regina rocked the baby to sleep. By the time Christian came through the door, Elizabeth and her sister were in a deep conversation about the beautiful new dress material just having arrived at Kiel's General Store.

"I couldn't imagine who was visiting," Christian remarked as he took off his coat, hanging it on the hook next to Conrad's. "You've got a new wagon, Conrad."

"Yes, the old one plus a table that I constructed bought me this new one," he smiled.

Silence permeated the room, and Chris thought that he detected an uneasiness.

"Is everything okay?" he asked, hesitantly.

Regina quickly glanced up at Conrad who in turn looked at Elizabeth who seemed to be fidgeting in her chair.

Finally, she answered, "I told them about America, Christian. I hope that you're not angry," she added quickly." She paused, waiting for Chris to comment. When he didn't she added, "They want to come along."

"Is that true?" Chris asked, a bit shocked as he attempted to digest this latest news. "I didn't realize that you were so upset with things in Germany.

Financially, you seem to be doing well, Conrad. You have a trade, and I've never heard you complain about the economics or politics."

"The shoemaking business is declining just like everything else, Chris. I think most Germans are upset — at least, the common folks. People can't afford to buy anything. Regina and I have discussed the prospect of going to American, but with just Fredrich there to help, it would be rough. He's not in the shoemaking business," Conrad said with a grin.

The tense lines of worry in Christian's face relaxed for the first time since he mentioned to Elizabeth the prospect of going to America. Laugh lines formed in their place as Christian broke into a broad smile. He glanced at his wife whose eyes reflected total happiness.

"This would make Elizabeth and me very happy — having Regina and you with us. And, of course, Louisa is ready to leave as well."

"Yes, Elizabeth told us. We'll all replant ourselves in the New World, and our children will have an opportunity for education and a good job someday. We won't have to worry about their futures."

Elizabeth had handed Chris a bowl of hot soup as she went to the door to call the children. Having just taken the freshly baked bread from the oven, the room was drenched with the delicious smell of pastry. Regina got up to set the table but first stopped the children to wipe their hands as they bound through the door in a fit of laughter.

As she grabbed her son, Christoph, who was trying to wiggle free from the washing, Regina added, "And don't forget freedom to worship as we wish. None of us have ever fully known that privilege."

With little Maria awake and crying from the cradle, Regina handed the damp cloth to Elizabeth and dropped the topic as the men continued to discuss with excitement the plans that were being formulated — amazing plans that would mean a new, enriched future for all of them.

Six

THE PASSING OF SOPHIA POLLMANN

The next day as Chris arose before the sun and slipped into his work clothes, he heard voices coming from the living room. One voice was Elizabeth's, but the other voice he didn't recognize. As he opened the door, he saw Dr. Schneider standing near the fire, speaking softly so as not to wake the children.

"Your ma's worse, Christian," Elizabeth said as he got within earshot. "Doc just left your parents' place, and your pa asked him to stop here because he doesn't want to leave her side."

Chris felt a growing lump in his throat and a tightening in his chest as he asked, "What's wrong exactly, Doc?"

"Pneumonia, I'd say. I left a poultice of herbs, but it sounds as if both lungs are full already, Chris. I'm sorry."

Chris was silent, and as his face paled at the news, Elizabeth reached for his hand.

"Go on, Chris. I'll tend to the chores."

Without hesitation, Christian grabbed his jacket from the hook near the door and headed for the barn to saddle Ole Red. A misty fog again covered the land as Chris made his way to his parents' house. With his mind as foggy as the countryside, he tried to recollect when he had last gone to visit his mother. Maybe ten days ago — she was ill, but she wasn't dying. He knew there was no certain cure for pneumonia, but it could sometimes be stopped with a combination of herbs — hyssops, rosemary, coltsfoot, and mullein — if it were caught early. If an herbal cough syrup could be administered when the infection began, the mucous might be broken up. But Chris knew that his mother had had a fever and constant cough for two weeks. Despite his silent prayers and attempts to convince himself that his mother would recover, deep in his heart he believed that it was too late.

As Chris neared the Pollmann homestead, he saw a dim light radiating from the living room and downstairs bedroom windows. The two-story house had once housed the nine-member family. As the Pollmanns grew, so did the house — Heinrich added rooms to the structure, eventually turning it into a four-bedroom home. Now, it seemed dark and foreboding with only the faintly lighted windows.

Even before he entered the house, he could smell the eucalyptus steam coming from the pot on the fire. As one pot cooled down in the bedroom, it was replaced by another hot pot emitting eucalyptus vapors. A quiet had settled over the house as Katherine and August — the two children still living at home — sat at the table in the dining room, staring into the nearby fire. Managing a faint smile as she saw her brother enter, Katherine — a calico apron covering her checked gingham dress — rose to take the cool pot from her father, exchanging it for a hot one.

A ribbon of light shown from the bedroom door, which was slightly ajar, as Chris entered the bedroom behind his father. He heard his mother's labored breathing as she tried to suck air into her mucous-filled lungs. Charlotte sat next to her mother on the bed, applying a poultice consisting of mutton fat, pecacuanha wine, and hot milk to her chest.

With dark circles under her eyes, Charlotte obviously had had little sleep the past two weeks. Strands of blonde hair fell into her eyes, and she tried to brush them back into her bun. As her eyes met Christian's, he made a swift motion with his hand, signaling her to leave and rest. With a quick shake of her head, Christian realized that Charlotte was not going to depart from her mother's side.

His glance fell on the edge of the bed where he saw a Bible, lying partially covered by the blanket. Probably — at their mother's request — Charlotte had been reading passages to her for strength and comfort. Sophia was clever even in her stupor — the passages were more for her family who were grieving than for her who was suffering. She knew that she would soon be passing into eternity, leaving her husband, children, and grandchildren to continue in a world filled with chaos, tribulation, and war. They would need the strength and courage to go forward; whereas, she would be safe with her Savior.

"Ma, it's Christian," he whispered, taking her feverish hand. A spasm of coughing followed as she tried to speak to him.

"Don't talk, Ma."

Her usually carefully combed brown hair lay in sweated strands on the pillow. Her once-beautiful face now contained sunken eyes and dry, cracked lips, leaving Christian with lost hope for her recovery. He wanted to scream out to her not to go, and he muffled a sob that nearly escaped from his lips.

"Here's some ginger tea," Charlotte said, lifting the cup to her mother's lips, and Heinrich placed the pot with renewed vapors next to the bed.

Charlotte and Heinrich seemed calm, but Christian believed it was actually exhaustion plus a firm resolution that this strongly religious woman was leaving her earthly home and going to the place that she most wanted to be.

Chris sat quietly holding her hand, as Charlotte finally retreated to the chair in the corner, allowing Chris an isolated moment alone with his mother. He watched the candle cast giant shadows onto the walls and thoughts of happier by-gone days in this room drifted through his mind — remembrances of sitting on his mother's bed as she read stories to him and his siblings. A nightly ritual, all the Pollmann family rallied for the best place on the bed, closest to their mother.

Fever followed by chills continued all day, and when Chris didn't return home by late afternoon, Elizabeth bundled the girls and hitched the wagon. By early evening, all of the children and spouses — except Fredrich, of course — and grandchildren had quietly filed into the home, taking turns entering the closed bedroom and speaking softly to Sophia. In and out of consciousness, she sometimes recognized the loved one at her bedside, but often as not her eyes were vacant and the coughing continued relentlessly.

A pot of broth and vegetables was kept on the fire although most had no appetite and sat silently praying or reading aloud some of Sophia's favorite Bible verses as the night waned on.

Around midnight, Chris decided to get some air. The children, whose parents were still sitting vigil, were on pallets on the floor, sound asleep. Chris envied them — all having carefree minds and possessing only problems that could be solved by their imaginations. He opened the door as the brisk February air hit him in the face, forcing him into the reality of the moment.

A myriad of stars shown above, reflecting a clear, brilliant sky. A beautiful night for someone to pass from this earthly life to eternity, Chris thought. He lost track of time as he stood under God's heavens — adorned not only with stars but also with a full, golden moon. How often as a child he and Charlotte had sat under the cover of a star-studded sky, singing and laughing until they were called to bed.

"Chris." The door had opened so quietly that he hadn't heard it. "Come quickly."

It was Charlotte. Her demeanor was calm, but tears streaked her cheeks as she took Christian's hand, leading him back into a world in which he didn't want to go.

It seemed different as he entered the bedroom. Warm from the steamy pot, the air smelled different. People say that a person can smell death, and Christian knew now exactly what they meant. It was a pungent odor, and a soft death rattle sounded from his mother's chest. Her eyes were closed, and she still struggled for each breath, but her facial expression had taken on a peaceful, more serene look.

"Ma, can you hear me?" He stroked his mother's clammy forehead and talked softly to her, knowing the sense of hearing would be the last to go.

Each loved one took his or her place next to Sophia Pollmann during her last earthly moments, and as the sun started to rise on the new day of February 29, 1852, Sophia Elizabeth Dorthea Pollmann passed into eternity.

Christian wanted to think of it as an end to physical life and a celebration into spiritual life, but still his heart was full with loss as he bent to kiss her moist, cold forehead. The kind, gentle woman who had nursed him, bandaged his scrapes, mended his clothes, and kissed away his problems was gone from him. It was something he hadn't imagined — others passed but not his mother.

Each person experienced his own personal grief on that clear, bright February morning. By midday, Charlotte, Christina, and Katherine had bathed Sophia and dressed her in her Sunday best, awaiting the friends, neighbors, and relatives to come view her body for a last time.

Seven

SCHWALENBERG

The weeks faded into early spring as the Pollmanns began preparation for departure. It had been difficult for Christian and his siblings to accept the fact that their beloved mother was gone. Katherine now became the housekeeper and cook for her father and brother. So much like her mother, Katherine had always shared special moments with Sophia. Katherine now was more quiet and reserved than usual, and Christian knew that her heart was breaking at the loss of not only her mother but also her dearest friend. With Sophia gone, Christian attempted to talk his father into going to America, too, but he resisted.

"Maybe later after you're settled, son," Heinrich said. "August and Katherine need stability right now — not a move to America."

Elizabeth's other sister, Lena, however, was wide-eyed at the idea. Unmarried at age 19, she was full of vim and vigor and eager for adventure. For Lena, exuberance and America could be whispered together in one sentence, and they played off one another in a way that Lena was thoroughly intrigued.

"Would I be a burden?" she quickly questioned. "I'd be the only one unmarried with no one to support me."

"Nonsense. How could you be a burden?" Elizabeth chided her. "You can help with the children on the boat, and there's sure to be a job just waiting for you in Illinois. And you can live with either Regina and Conrad or with us if you wish."

For Lena, then, it was settled — she was going.

Elizabeth's fear had been telling her parents, which the three sisters did soon after Lena's decision. Losing three girls to the New World would be difficult, but the Haas' religious strength was projected as they displayed excitement — outwardly at least — at a new future for their children.

Johann — much more receptive than his wife — promised to consider the prospect of eventually joining the girls in Illinois, and his comments at least made departure easier for Elizabeth and her sisters.

* * * * *

It was mandatory for the head of each household to make a trip to the town hall in Schwalenberg — a nearby village — to obtain rights of passage for the entire family who would be voyaging to America. Early the next Wednesday morning, Conrad and Christian started out in Conrad's wagon over the still snow-covered mountains of Lipperland. The two men would act as heads of household for all the women and children going on the voyage, and Christian found that he made the trip with mixed emotions.

Although he was anxious to pursue a new life, he still clung to the land of his childhood. He and his father had made weekly journeys to Schwalenberg when he was a child helping his father on the farm. It was always a reprieve from work and a real treat to go to the beautiful village of half-timbered houses where they could participate in the farmers' market located next to the town hall.

Intricate carvings along with the unique and decorative designs were displayed on the parapets of these sixteenth-century buildings of Schwalenberg. Christian wondered if America would possess such ornately ornamented and beautifully gabled facades as these structures, which still displayed the wealth that had been enjoyed in the golden era of the 1700s. The splendid half-timbered structures seemed perfect against the idyllic backdrop of the green fields, tranquil ponds, blue skies, and rolling mountains of Lipperland.

The medieval castle of the thirteenth-century town was nestled on the steep slope overlooking the picturesque village — a place in which time seemed to stand still. Occasionally, Heinrich would take Christian to the castle to see the fantastic view of Lipperland.

Christian had always loved the farmers' market, which lasted until noon each Friday in Schwalenberg, and after he and his father were finished selling their produce, Heinrich would always suggest that they have a bite to eat and something to drink at the Malkasten.

The village's most popular pub, the Malkasten, had been built in 1700, and its half-timbered structure had one side that was uniquely painted with whimsical characters who were eating, drinking, and dancing. Tables and benches filled the large interior of the pub where people gathered to eat a brat and drink a glass of ale before returning to work. It was a magical time for Christian to join his father, and he sat, ate, laughed, and drank with all of the grownups, who were doing business that day in Schwalenberg.

Conrad and Christian spent several hours in the town hall, filling out papers for the voyage to America and changing rooms, only to find another stack of documents to complete. Certification of personal information of each person was necessary, along with papers showing that the family had money for passage with a minimum amount of money to start in the New World. Papers had to be completed in order that trunks with necessary articles could be sent ahead of the ship, and complicated documents showing ownership of land and commodities had to be released. The stack of papers was mind boggling, and by late afternoon, Conrad and Christian were ready to visit the Malkasten before the trek home.

A German band of five men were playing as the two entered the smoky pub, and the crowd was already raucous as they sang, danced, and clapped in time to the German polkas. For an hour, Christian and Conrad relaxed and joined in the festivities before leaving at the dusky hour of 6 o'clock. The horse had been rested and fed at the livery, and the two weary travelers boarded the wagon to make their way back along the well-traveled roads leading to Hummersen.

Eight

FALKENHAGEN'S EVANGELICAL CHURCH

With only a few weeks left before departure, Christian found there was not enough time to accomplish all he had to do. The trunks were packed with necessities and taken by a neighbor to Minden where they were put aboard a boat on their way to Bremerhaven. There a ship waited, taking cargo to the American Cargo Company, located in New York City. From New York, the trunks would board a train bound for the Midwest, arriving perhaps a month later in Illinois.

As the days passed, Christian found he was working late into the night to get his family ready. Even then, he couldn't sleep well as his mind stirred with restless thoughts of the upcoming voyage and the move to a foreign land, which seemed evermore frightening with each passing day. Prayer was his only comfort, and his church in Falkenhagen seemed the only sanctuary to calm his ever-rising fears.

The Thursday before departure, Christian slept little — two hours at the most — and finally at 4 o'clock, he slipped quietly into his clothes, carrying his boots to the living room so as not to waken Elizabeth. Normally, she awoke when her husband stirred, but that morning she seemed dead to the world. Christian's wish was to make a final walk through his beloved village, the

Lipperland countryside, and go to Falkenhagen's church before they departed — and he wanted to walk alone to reminisce bygone days.

Silently opening the outside door, he took a lantern and pulled on his coat against the March wind. The flat valley of farmland gave way to the mountains outside of Hummersen, which were still not visible in the early morning hours. Christian slowly strolled through the village of Hummersen that he had called home for 25 years. The narrow cobblestone streets housed half-timbered structures similar to Schwalenberg's, and half a dozen shops and stores lined one small alleyway leading out of town. Soon Christian was in the rural area, on a path leading to Falkenhagen.

The Lipperland area lay embedded in forests, mountain ranges, tranquil ponds, and silvery rivers — an oasis of natural beauty. Christian entered the deep forest, which led the way towards the only church that he had ever known. A few birds already had begun their wake-up calls as he walked the well-trod path that he knew so well. Every Sunday — rain, sleet, snow, or sun — the Pollmanns traveled together as a family to worship. Only illness would keep a family member home, and Christian could count on one hand the number of times he had remained in bed because of ill health.

On a constant upward incline over the mountain, the forest thickened so that even in the daylight, the sun's rays couldn't penetrate the depth of the trees. It was especially cold in the shaded, darkened path under the trees clumped so close together that it was difficult to walk comfortably through the forest — it was imperative to stay on the path. Glad that he had brought the lantern, Christian held it close to the path for twenty minutes until the forest thinned, and the first golden rays showed over the mountaintop in the distance. As the steeple appeared, Christian turned off the main road onto a small, winding path that eventually led around the side of the church — the trail that he and his siblings used to run to see who could be first to reach the entrance.

As he approached the huge, oaken door at the front of the church built in 1248, Christian took the handle and opened it, revealing the beautiful sanctuary, cold and damp from the chilled winter weather. How often he had sat in the quiet of this chamber with the high-arched cathedral ceilings.

The sun played with the stained glass colors of the windows, and Christian walked to the front pew so as to focus on the large, round oaken pulpit, which seemed to dwarf the church. To the right side was the balcony, which allowed the choir to sit above the people and radiate their beautiful tones over the congregation. Tears welled in his eyes as Christian knew that he would not see the sanctuary again, and he stared at the benches located under the three stained glass windows where his father sat each Sunday as an elder.

"Lord, bless and guard my family on the forthcoming voyage. Be with us throughout our struggles in the New World," he whispered.

He sat silently, cementing into his mind the incredible church from every possible view. It was a beautiful sanctuary — old but simple and a place that had held the Pollmann family on Sundays for generations. After a time, Christian rose from the narrow wooden pew and walked to the small side room in which he had participated in confirmation. So many hours had been spent studying God's word in that tiny chamber and so much knowledge had been passed from the pastor to the confirmands. For Christian, it had always been a blessing to be in church and part of God's family. He knew that he would miss the peace and tranquility, which he continually found in the solitude of Falkenhagen's church.

By now, light flooded the church, and Christian returned to the interior room, walking down the aisle a final time. His eyes focused on the golden organ pipes, which filled the upper rear of the church. Christian loved the organ music as it echoed and reverberated throughout the sanctuary on Sunday mornings. He only hoped that the church in Illinois would house as splendid a pipe organ as the one in this church.

With a glance over his shoulder, Christian looked for a last time at the three vertical strained glass windows in the front of the church — the middle one beautifully displaying Christ's suffering on the cross. They were magnificent, especially as the morning sun sprayed its light on them. He opened the door to a light mist as he continued to the church cemetery. His mother's grave had had no chance to receive planted flowers, which he knew his father would tend to as soon as spring sprung. He knelt, though, at the tombstone.

"Sophia Elizabeth Dorthea Kiel Pollmann, Geb. 2 June 1815, D. 29 Feb. 1852."

Silently, Christian prayed to his mother and wished he could touch her hand one last time or place a kiss on her cheek. Knowing that he carried his mother in his heart wherever he went, he sat on the damp ground with his hands touching the cold granite of her tombstone. Finally, with peace in his heart, he rose to take the familiar path leading through the forest toward Hummersen.

Rays of sunlight lit the darkened forest path now, and as Christian reached his village by 8 o'clock, the mist had stopped, and people were already busy in Hummersen as farmers brought their products to be sold or traded. Christian nodded a greeting to each of them as he made his way home.

Seeing smoke spiraling from the chimney of the small rural home, he knew Elizabeth had been up several hours already. He hoped she had guessed he had been walking, something he often did when he was restless.

"Good morning, Chris. You've been out for a stroll?" Elizabeth remarked as he entered the door.

"Yes. I wanted to go alone — a final walk to Falkenhagen."

"I assumed as much," she smiled. "Please, sit down by the fire, and I'll get coffee and bread. You must be chilled."

He sat and taking the Bible from the table, he let it fall open to his favorite verse — The Twenty-third Psalm.

"The Lord is my shepherd. I shall not want. He makes me lie down in green pastures. He leads me beside quiet waters. He restores my soul....Even though I walk through the valley of the shadow of death, I will fear no evil, for you are with me....Surely goodness and love will follow me all the days of my life, and I will dwell in the house of the Lord forever."

Christian wondered what valleys of death he would encounter in the New World. He reminded himself, though, that Jesus always had his rod and staff to protect him; there would also be green pastures and quiet waters after the tribulations; and that the Lord's goodness and love would always be with his family.

Christian closed the Bible and shut his eyes. Trying to cement into his mind the sights of the mountains, forests, and paths leading to Falkenhagen's church, he knew that he'd never forget. These were childhood memories that would remain in his heart forever.

Nine

THE LAST NIGHT AT THE HOMESTEAD

With their belongings all sold — the Pollmanns returned to their homestead to spend the last few days before departure. With trunks packed with necessities and previously sent abroad, the Pollmanns and their children awaited this day — March 10 — to depart for the northern city of Bremen. Hopefully, by the end of the week, they'd be in Bremerhaven — the harbor — ready to leave for America.

The morning of March 10 had not yet dawned when Christian rolled over to find Elizabeth already gone down to the kitchen. He had slept very little but dozed off sometime after 3 o'clock in the morning, and shortly thereafter, his wife had slipped out of bed, descending the stairs to the kitchen. Margaretha and Anna-Marie — bundled in pallets on the floor — had finally settled down near midnight. Louisa and her children occupied one of the other upstairs bedrooms — the room that once had been Heinrich and Sophia's. Unable to return to that bedroom since Sophia's death, Heinrich had opted to sleep in the downstairs bedroom. Until now, their bedroom had remained untouched for the last six weeks.

As Christian lay savoring the last few minutes in the home in which he had grown up, his thoughts drifted to a story told by Ludwig Muller, to whom he had sold his last piece of farm equipment. Afraid to tell Elizabeth, he had kept the story to himself, attempting to block it even from his own mind.

In 1816, some of Muller's ancestors — along with many other Germans — fell under the spell of "emigration fever," wanting desperately to go to America. Possessing little more than the clothes on their backs, the Mullers and some of their friends — seven families in all — abandoned their farms, shops, and homes, and began the long journey to the New World. They dreamed of fertile farmlands, lush pastures, rivers and lakes full of fish, and thick green forests. Walking to the Rhine River, the Germans boarded a barge to Amsterdam, Holland. Along the way, they encountered a torrent of shaggy, starving refugees from all over Europe, all hopeful of a bright, new future in America. Arriving in Amsterdam, the Germans found 200,000 refugees living in deep poverty, awaiting vessels bound for America. With a shortage of ships able to make such a long voyage, the few boats that could sail — and even they were ill-prepared for such a trip — were crammed with hundreds of passengers.

The seven German families were among the dozens of refugees who bought tickets at a warehouse on Nieuwezijds Voorburgwal Canal in Amsterdam with a promise to sail on the *Rudolph* the next day. Crossing the Zuiderzee to the deep-water port on the outskirts of Amsterdam, the Germans stood looking with horror at the *Rudolph*. She was a run down, antiquated hulk with rotting sails and a splintered wooden deck. Rather than a crew to greet them, they were met on board with foul smells and devastating sights. After days of waiting for the departure of the ship, the Germans — by then joined by more desperate refugees — were told that the *Rudolph* wouldn't sail. Depression and horror seized the penniless emigrants as they tried to fathom what to do next.

With all of their money gone, the seven German families — and now hundreds of other Europeans — searched in desperation for transportation over the Atlantic. A particular — rather shifty — merchant of Amsterdam had three ships that offered voyage to the New World. With no money to buy tickets, the emigrants were destitute, but the merchant had a suggestion to solve the problem. Each of the seven families would receive a document to sign — a redemption agreement. The emigrants could travel free to America; however, a high cost awaited them in New Orleans. They would be sold into servitude. Although it seemed like an incredibly awful, unthinkable idea, the German refugees — trapped in poverty for weeks with no money and already stripped of their dignity — had no choice but to sign.

Sickness, suicide, and death followed the refugees on those well-known "coffin ships," and by the time New Orleans was in view, the passengers were crazed with hunger and thirst as well as weakened with illness, depression, and hopelessness.

When the ships went into port, throngs of noisy farmers, merchants, and tradesmen pushed to view "the white slaves." Bargaining began, conducted by the captain of each ship. Interest and welfare of each German family was null — the captain wanted the highest price regardless if families were kept together or not. The negotiations were made in a language the immigrants didn't understand, and they were forced to sign an indenture in words they couldn't read. It was a horrible catastrophe for the German families who set out months before expecting to find a bright, hopeful future in the New World.

Christian lay in bed this March morn before leaving the village of Hummersen, thinking of those seven German families who anticipated everything that he was expecting. It was a story he couldn't tell with his wife, but one that he knew he could discuss only with his God.

Silently, he prayed, "Dear Lord, safeguard my family from danger and disaster. Give us strength to endure the hardships which are sure to occur, but bless us with the knowledge and understanding to work out the problems — always for your benefit, Lord."

Again, Christian was depending on the strong faith passed on by his mother. Although Sophia was gone, that part of her could never be taken from him, and he clung to it tenaciously. His mind wandered to the trunk that he had packed a week before and which had already sailed for America. With little room for anything but necessities, Christian had tenderly wrapped two priceless pictures that his mother had given him when he married. They were treasures — luxuries — but to Christian they were considered "necessities," and Elizabeth hadn't argued. One read, "Without the Holy Cross there is no Salvation," and the other had a golden cross and crown delicately placed in the center, and it read, "Without the Holy Cross there is no Crown." Handed down from Sophia's mother, the pictures should have gone to Georg, the eldest, but Sophia had wanted Christian — sometimes thought to be her favorite — to have them, and on the day that he and Elizabeth said their vows, Sophia handed them the wrapped package.

The sun was just starting to peak over the horizon as Christian Pollmann felt the cold floor on his bare feet. It must be 4 o'clock, he thought, which meant that they had a little over two hours to get ready for travel to Minden where they'd catch the train bound for Bremen. Quietly, he tiptoed from the room so as not to wake the children.

Lena, Regina, and her family had stayed with their parents this last night. Talking, singing, and eating until near midnight, they too were awake by 4 o'clock, preparing for their departure. The families had arranged to leave at 6 o'clock, taking four boats up the Weser River to Minden, hoping that this would allow ample time to catch the 10 o'clock train.

Already there was talking in the kitchen as Chris softly closed the bedroom door. Louisa and Elizabeth had breakfast started, and the smell of strong, German coffee filtered up the stairs. Georg had come with his family the previous night for final goodbyes, but Charlotte and Christina saved their farewells for this last morning. Heinrich sat at the table, a bit bent as if carrying a burden too heavy, and with a look of despair showing in his eyes. Christian held to the hope that his father would come to America soon.

Chris remembered their conversation of the previous week which was met with resignation by his father, and he hoped that letters from America would help convince Katherine, August, Charlotte with her husband, and his father to join them once they were settled. If not, he realized this would be the last time he'd see his father. Standing silently on the stairs — unnoticed — Chris cemented the image of Heinrich Pollmann into his mind. Heinrich had been a strong, loving father, and together with Sophia, they had provided a very sound, solid family structure in which to raise seven children. Christian felt blessed that he had had 25 years with his parents, and now as he stood looking at his father, he felt he would never be the man that he saw before him. Unbeknownst to Christian, however, the upcoming years in the New World would mold him into a man with strength, knowledge, and wisdom beyond his years, and God would use him to fulfill some of His most important, best-laid plans.

Ten

HUMMERSEN TO BREMEN

By 6 o'clock, the four boats were carefully packed with the family's rucksacks as some of Heinrich's friends took their places at the oars. The partings were swept with grief and new-sprung uncertainty. Christian had anticipated this moment, but reality hit hard as he hugged the sister to whom he was most closely bound. Charlotte unsuccessfully choked back tears as she tore herself away from Christian, and the four siblings who were left behind waved as the boats drifted out of sight.

The ride to Minden was interspersed with chatter, mixed with awkward silences. Johann and Anna Haas — in one boat with Regina, Lena, and Elizabeth — were losing all three of their children to the New World, and Anna was putting up a brave front. With God as her strength, she bore her usual smile and spoke with genuine optimism to her children and grandchildren. Heinrich — riding next to Christian , Margaretha, and Anna-Marie — felt an emptiness close to that of losing Sophia. Two sons, two daughters-in-law, and five grandchildren were all being swallowed by the New World, and he hoped he was not too old and set in his ways to adjust to this circumstance, which presently seemed too imposing to endure.

Sophia had always possessed such closeness to God, acquiring all the fortitude and stability that stemmed from such a relationship. As much as

Heinrich struggled to gain the same proximity, he always felt he fell short. Silently, now, he sat in the boat which drifted down the Weser River between Hummersen and Minden, and he prayed for peace as well as courage to brave this seemingly insurmountable situation.

Elizabeth had recurring thoughts of skepticism and concern. They were taking all of their children to an untamed frontier, and she fought the turbulent thoughts and doubts. She knew she wasn't the only one praying silently as intermittently one and then the other sister would temporarily fall silent.

Conrad was in one boat with his children, and he attempted to play games with them to occupy their minds. Louisa — in the fourth boat — tried to pass time singing to her three children. She had often done that with her children during frightening storms, and it just seemed appropriate now. Of all the travelers, they seemed least anxious of the upcoming journey as they anticipated the reunion with their father.

Christian noted that the March air was brisk and the unplowed fields were not only barren but also water logged from the spring thaw. With heavy snows in the dead of winter and too much rain the past month, farming conditions looked similar to the previous year — too wet and too cold for a good growing season and no hope for an ample harvest.

Still, Christian surveyed the only land that he had ever known — the rolling acres outside of Hummersen, which plummeted into the Egge and Weser mountains and fell into valleys of green, lush pastureland. He thought of his favorite places in Lipperland — Bad Pyrmont and Bad Salzuflen with their huge country parks and healing baths, Koterberg's highest mountain in the area providing the most spectacular panorama of northern Germany, and the grottos, caves, and high chapel dating to the twelfth century in Externsteine. Most importantly, Chris knew he'd miss Luegde and the ancient Lenten tradition of burning the six wheels of oaken straw at break of dawn on Easter morning. Every year, Chris and his family, along with hundreds of other visitors, participated in the ancient Easter ritual.

As he sat in the boat, Christian's thoughts again returned to his childhood days in Hummersen. With the fields dotted with large oak trees and acres amass with kaleidoscopic colors — Queen Anne's white lace, purple coneflowers, and yellow buttercups — he had loved to roam through the waist-high grasses. Taking his fishing pole to the Weser River, Christian, Fredrich, and Charlotte would spend a Sunday afternoon in the shade of a giant old maple tree, catching catfish for the Pollmann supper table. Sometimes the Dully children would join them, and the five youngsters would pass the lazy afternoon fishing, singing, and eating berries from the nearby blackberry bushes.

Proudly, Christian and his siblings would walk home, holding a string of a dozen fish to feed the family that evening. They would meander through the fields — the boys whistling a German folk tune while Charlotte would dance and whirl, stopping momentarily to pick wild flowers for her mother.

"Christian." The voice of his mother seemed a million kilometers away. "This is a fine catch," she'd say as he entered the door and handed his mother the string of fish.

"I'll skin the catfish, Ma. Wanted to show them to you first," he'd say as he grinned proudly.

Charlotte would push her way past Christian, thrusting a fistful of blue forget-me-nots and yellow black-eyed susans at her mother.

"How beautiful, sweetheart. thank you," Sophia would say, clutching the flowers. "And the sweet williams and evening primroses that you brought in a few days ago are just starting to wilt. These will look beautiful on the table tonight."

"Christian." Again the voice was faint — this time, though, it was his father's, and it drew him from his reverie as they neared the dock of Minden. "It looks as if the train's already in the station. You better hurry."

Quickly, the boats were tied to the docks, and everyone grabbed a rucksack. Already the conductor's deep voice was calling "All aboard" and so final farewells were — perhaps fortunately — expedited. All that was going to be said had been expressed at breakfast or on the journey to Minden, and so, in reality, they didn't need long goodbyes.

By the time the fourteen travelers found their designated seats, the conductor made his last call to the passengers, and the train's whistle screamed its goodbye to Minden. With a jerk, it started to roll, and the eight children began their first journey on a locomotive. Entranced by this new-found adventure, they were given the best seats by the windows, and they stared wide-eyed and open-mouthed as the big black engine snorted immense amounts of dark smoke from its chimney, and they slowly chugged their way out of the station.

What a contraption this locomotive of the 1800s was with antiquated cylinders, pistons, rods, axes, and wheels, and driven by a boiler and furnace, which emitted combustion into a tall chimney. But is was an amazing invention for the nineteenth century, and the children were speechless by the six-ton piece of machinery.

As they huffed and puffed over the countryside — heading north towards Bremen — the Haas and Pollmann families were all glued to the windows as fields of wildflowers were just starting to bloom — white shasta daisies, yellow evening primrose, purple sweet williams, and golden lupine.

Elizabeth's favorite flower was bachelor buttons — the bluest blossom in the flower kingdom — and as she sat looking at the beginnings of colorful fields, she remembered one area near her childhood home, which each year was a lush carpet of blue, dancing under the golden summer sun. Elizabeth had often picked bachelor buttons for her mother when she was a little girl. When she finally arrived home, sometimes her bouquet was half wilted, as she clutched it tightly in her sweaty hand, but Anna was always delighted and displayed the flowers proudly in a glass in the center of the dining table.

Maybe it was the departure from one of the only villages that they had ever known, but the Haas sisters found themselves reminiscing their childhood memories. Eventually, the three girls began to talk about their favorite holiday — Christmas. Giggling like children, the sisters remembered the many joyous years of celebrating Christ's birth.

Lighting the Advent wreath was always a ceremony that the Haas family awaited. With each new Sunday, another candle was lit, and a gilt paper star was added to the Christmas wreath. The girls giggled with glee as the Advent calendar appeared. Each day a new window of the calendar was opened, revealing a delicious piece of German chocolate as the girls divided it three ways and savored the rich sweetness of the candy.

And the Christmas markets! Elizabeth was already starting to laugh as she remembered a market when she was seven or eight years old.

"It was snowing that beautiful white, wet snow that sticks to everything — roofs, tree branches, and noses," she smiled. "The trees on the road to Detmold were totally drenched in white purity. It was spectacular."

"How did we get to Detmold?" Lena asked.

"By wagon. I must have been seven because you were a baby, Lena. Do you remember, Regina?"

"Yes, of course. It must have been around 1843. We left early and almost didn't go at all because of the snowstorm the previous night. I remember that scenery — it was amazing," Regina answered.

"We spent the day going from stall to stall, buying charming little wooden Christmas ornaments, frosted gingerbread cookies, and sugary marzipan," Elizabeth continued. "We'd duck into an enclosed building from time to time to warm up at the fire and drink hot chocolate. German bands were playing in the Christmas tents and carolers strolled among the stalls singing the old traditional Christmas songs."

"I remember all of that because I'd never seen anything like that ever," Regina added, her eyes gleaming at the thought of that magical day.

"Well, I remember that that year I had my heart set on a delicate wooden toy made by a man living near the Black Forest. This toy maker brought his wares to various Christmas markets around Germany, and this particular year he was in Detmold," Elizabeth explained.

"What was the toy? Do you still have it?" Lena asked two questions in succession, eager to hear more.

"Well, the toy was an intricately carved German doll whose arms and legs moved. And to answer your second question, no, I don't have it."

Regina remembered the incident and was stifling a laugh as Elizabeth continued.

"I went back to that stall four or five times that day, begging Pa to buy me the doll. It was tiny — could fit into my hand — and Pa said it was silly, useless, and a waste of money. Finally, when we were about ready to leave, Ma talked him into getting it for me. I was speechless. The tiny, facial features were intricately carved and her dirndl, blouse, and shoes were all brightly painted. Brown hair was tucked under her lace hat, and she looked like a fairy princess to me."

When Elizabeth paused, Lena's eyes went from Regina to Elizabeth. "Well, go on; what happened?" Lena insisted.

"As we were ready to leave, it had started to snow again," Elizabeth continued. "A marching band had come around the corner and continued down the main street of the Christmas Market. I had stopped to admire some glass ornaments in a stall, and as I ran to catch up with Ma and Pa, I slipped on the wet snow. Down went my wooden doll, and as my precious toy hit the ground, so did the drummer's big, black boot."

"Oh, no," said Lena, unable to contain her giggle.

I nodded. "I tried to pick up the pieces, but she was smashed. I've never forgiven that drummer." Elizabeth finally allowed herself to laugh. "You know, it feels good to finally say that I have never forgiven that clumsy drummer with his big old boot. He never even knew that he had stepped on my beautiful doll. He just kept walking."

The three girls laughed, and the children, who had been quietly listening, joined in, unable to believe that their Aunt Elizabeth had been a child just like them with feelings as fragile as theirs.

* * * * *

Christian seemed entranced in the countryside and Conrad's eyes were closed, catching a much-needed nap. Louisa talked softly to the children as they played finger games so the Haas girls continued to reminisce about their joyous Christmas days. They remembered the epitome of Christmas — Christmas Eve — when the Haas family dressed in their finest and made the trek into Falkenhagen for church service. Pulled out for the special occasion were velvet or taffeta dresses, altered either bigger or smaller to fit one of the girls that Christmas. Hats, scarves, and muffs adorn the plain wool winter coats, and the girls felt like princesses.

The mountain road leading to Falkenhagen was always snow-covered at that time of year, and a steady line of lanterns lit the way as millions of flakes fell from the sky, making it a truly magical journey. The dense forest looked as if it had been dipped in white chocolate as the clumps of snow clung to every branch and twig. As the family entered the sanctuary, nothing could surpass the joy of that eve with the main chamber decorated with fir trees, bells, candles, and wreaths. The Christmas choir's clear, rich voices could be heard even before the congregation got to the church as they sang *O Little Town of Bethlehem, Away in a Manger, Oh Come All Ye Faithful,* and *Silent Night.* Accompanied by not only the vibrant pipe organ but also a harp, violin, and cello, the music reverberated off the walls of the sanctuary, echoing and re-echoing in the minds of the congregation as they came to worship the birth of the Christ child.

The service always contained the story of the first Christmas and was finalized with the taking of communion. As the service closed, each person walked down the aisle with an unlit candle, lighting it at the large white candle at the front of the church. Surrounded with a wreath of greenery and red holly berries, the candle commemorated Christ as the light of the world forever and always. It was the high point of the year for many Germans as they filed out into the snow-packed mountain roads to walk home, their lanterns again lighting the way.

The eager Haas children pulled at their parents' hands or ran ahead, too excited to wait. The splendid holiday feast and festivities awaited them at home — prepared for days in advance by their mother and grandmother. The two would work diligently for an entire week, baking lebkuchen, spekulatius, mince pie, and stollen. Germany potato pancakes, roast hog, spatzle (dumplings), kraut, metzelsuppe (soup with sausage), and wassail were all prepared and stored in the cold cellar to await Christmas Eve. The stove, oven, and fire were never left unattended that week, as a feast for royalty was being prepared.

It was the one night that the Haas children were not sent to bed early because they were allowed to feast until midnight. At that time Opa Haas would pick up his small Christmas drum, beating it merrily throughout the house as the entire family — biggest to smallest — followed him upstairs, through the halls, and around the corners until they came to the Christmas Tree Room. A small room — normally the sitting parlor — was turned into this special room, especially for Christmas Eve.

Earlier in the day, the Haas children had helped decorate the fir tree with candles, bells, paper ornaments, and garland. Now, with the candles magically lit and gifts heaped under the dazzling, fragrant fir tree, the Haas children stood awestruck at the door. Surely, St. Nicholas had snuck in while they were away at church and distributed gifts for the entire Haas family. As they filed in, carols were sung, finally ending with *Stille Nacht (Silent Night)* as the packages were finally ready to be opened.

Even though it was after midnight, excitement kept the Haas girls from sleeping, adrenalin pumping rapidly through their veins, and they begged their father to retell the legends of Christmas.

Johann would never deny the children the privilege of hearing the traditional Germany legends of Christmas as he started the first story.

"On the first Christmas when Christ was born, the Magi slowly walked though the village of Bethlehem, which was not so different than Hummersen. And, lo, all the winter trees were abloom as if it were springtime. The three Magi were astounded as they looked around because, after all, it was December, but it looked like May. Birds sang as they built their nests, warm breezes blew through the branches, and honeybees swarmed around their hives. Green leaves and beautiful white blossoms covered the trees, and the three Wisemen sat under a blossoming apple tree to view the beauty. It is because of this event — the green trees with white blossoms — that today we use the evergreen with lighted candles to commemorate that first Christmas."

Johann never told the girls that he added embellishment to the story — a little different each year — but the basis of the story was there, and the girls loved it.

Anna would always tell the second legend as the children gathered more closely around the foot of the evergreen.

"Martin Luther would bring a small fir tree into his house each Christmas Eve just for his little son. They would decorate it with dried berries strung on a string, paper ornaments, and bells. Then Luther would attach candles to the branches. Once lit, he would remind his son that the candles looked just as the starry heavens on that first silent Christmas Eve."

As the sisters finished reminiscing the Christmas legends, they felt the train slowing. Glancing out the window, they realized that they were nearing a large city. Bremen, Elizabeth thought. With all the chattering, the time had passed and they were already at their northern destination. Baby Maria had slept the entire way, and Anna-Marie lay cuddled in her Aunt Louisa's lap.

Bremen. Were they ready for this? The train was slowly rolling into the outskirts. All faces were now pressed against the train windows as they saw closely-squeezed houses — too many to be counted. From the hundreds of red chimneys, black smoke drifted upward, mixed with a light mist and fog from the river. Church spires pointed upward like fingers reaching toward a brighter place than Germany. Flocks of birds pin-wheeled in a frenzy around the church towers as the bells peeled clear, glorious sounds. Carts, stalls, stores, and people were crowded in and around the city center, and the Pollmann and Haas families were awestruck with wonder. It was a daunting sight.

Louisa glanced at Christian, hoping he wasn't overwhelmed. Seemingly, Chris was the leader of the group, and Louisa yearned for his strength and courage to carry her — and the rest of the family — through this arduous journey. His look was steady and constant, and Louisa tried to draw from his confidence.

Christian sat silently observing the scenery, and he realized that the others must be overwrought with fear and uncertainty in a strange, intimidating city like Bremen. Many years before, he had seen Bremen with his father and grandfather, and he remembered how staggering the sight could be — huge industrial warehouses crowding the waterfront, dozens of ships cramming the docks, and hundreds of people from all over Europe looking for transportation abroad. These shear numbers of homeless people, tattered and poverty-stricken, were horrifying.

"This is just the start, dear ones," Christian said as he turned to the wide-eyed youngsters. "We're going to be introduced to more big cities. Bremerhaven is bigger than Bremen, and then there will be New Orleans. I guess that it will be unbelievably huge — and in a foreign country!" Chris paused momentarily. "It's all a part of our exciting new life, though, and we need to be thankful for it." Christian grinned, trying to remain confident and steady.

"As long as you aren't afraid, Uncle Chris. You are our guide," little Karl commented as he sat on his uncle's lap.

Christian smiled back. "I want you — all of you — to remember one thing. I'm not your guide, really. The Lord is our guide — our guiding light. As long as He's not overwhelmed, we're safe. And He is never overwhelmed with anything. Always remember that."

The children all giggled as they shook their heads in agreement, and Christian believed that he saw his wife's face relax slightly and the corners of Regina's mouth curl into a faint smile.

Eleven

BREMEN

Slowly the train halted in the Bremen depot, and hesitantly the travelers exited in awe as they walked through the train station, carrying their rucksacks and holding tightly to their children's hands. Feeling woefully out of place among the people from all over Europe, seemingly speaking every language except German, the fourteen family members made their way to the depot doors leading into the heart of Bremen. A multitude of signs, buildings towering high over their heads, and muddy streets leading in all directions were daunting sights for people from a small village like Hummersen.

Directly in front of the family was a huge poster of a ship at sea. In big letters were times of departure as well as "Go to America for 100 Talers only."

"Are we taking that ship, Uncle Chris?" Elise asked, pointing to the sign.

"We'll see, Elise. There are many ships sailing. We have to take one that goes to New Orleans and has space for all of us. That's a job for Conrad and me to work on while you ladies and gentlemen," he said, pointing to her and the other youngsters, "enjoy the sights in the big city. Just look at those store windows over there."

Chris was pointing to a slew of stores, all sporting wide glass windows with new fashions that the girls had never seen.

"Where did all those clothes come from?" Margaretha cried. "Someone's mother must have spent a lot of time sewing."

Elizabeth grinned as she explained that store-bought clothes were made in factories, not at home. Trying to understand what she meant, the children just stared at Elizabeth.

"But, Ma, all the clothes in those windows would take all of the material that's in Kiel's General Store!" Margaretha continued.

"Yes, sweetheart, I guess they would." Elizabeth smiled, deciding not to pursue the topic that was unfathomable to the children.

Elizabeth glanced at Christian who was looking in the direction of the street in front of them.

"What are you thinking, Chris?"

"We need to find a place to stay. I wish Conrad and I could go searching and leave you ladies and children here, but I don't feel safe doing that."

"I don't think it's a good idea for us to stand here alone," Lena added.

"Can all of you can manage to come along then?" Chris asked.

"Yes, of course," they answered in unison.

Grabbing their bundles, the Pollmann and Haas families followed the street, which emptied into a wide boulevard, crowded with emigrants milling about with their rucksacks, boxes, and wagons heaped with possessions. Many of the people were ragged and tattered, looking as if they had been homeless and searching for passage to America for some time. Ahead of them were the boats that would take them to their next German destination — Bremerhaven.

Christian could see a large square in the distance, and it seemed to be full of street performers, something with which the children were not well acquainted. Once there had been jugglers and dancers in Detmold at the Christmas markets, but the performers that Christian could see ahead far surpassed those. Mimes and a flamboyant puppet show were taking place, and among other things was an organ grinder making music with the aid of a red-capped monkey. Tethered to his master with a long cord, the little brown monkey begged for coins with a small tarnished silver cup. When rewarded, he clapped his hands and did a somersault. With wide eyes, ferocious chattering, and huge grins, the monkey was successful getting money from the crowd of spectators. The children stood awestruck, and little Karl clapped with glee as the monkey seemed to be performing just for him.

"Are you looking for a room?" The voice came from an alley and was barely loud enough for Chris to hear above the music from the performers.

"A room?" Christian asked, looking at a rag-tag lad of ten or eleven years whose thin face seemed devoured by his large brown eyes. With dirty hands, he brushed his brown shaggy hair aside and nodded.

"Yes, a room. Are you emigrants looking for a place to stay?" He moved closer, and the rest of the family stopped to listen, their hopes building.

"Yes, do you know of some clean rooms?" Chris asked.

"Oh, yes, sir, I do. Frau Schmidt has the best rooms in town. They're cheap and close. Want to follow me?"

Christian looked at Conrad who nodded, and the adults tried to gather the children who were now thoroughly engrossed in the street performers.

"I want to see more, please," begged Karl who had gotten close enough to the monkey to shake hands.

"Maybe later," said Louisa. "We need to follow Uncle Chris right now, darling."

Pulling the children away was no easy task, and Christian — along with the others — followed the young boy who had started down the alley from where he first appeared. Christian tried to ask the lad some questions, but he seemed unwilling to carry on a conversation. Rather, he seemed intense on finding the correct street. The alley led into a boulevard, congested with a disarray of people, some of them carrying what seemed to be their bare worldly possessions. The noise was a deafening discord of calls, shouts, and cries of sellers hawking their wares at a local street market, and the emigrants were overwhelmed once again at the chaos of Bremen. Anna-Marie started to cry as Christian scooped her into his arms, and Margaretha clung tightly to her mother's hand. As Regina sheltered the baby tightly in a bundle in her arms, Conrad and Lena held tenaciously to the other youngsters' sweaty palms.

It was all they could do to keep up with the boy, who was now leading them through a muddy street, narrow and dark. Garbage was piled high and the stench was awful. Some homeless bodies covered with tattered blankets slept in the gutter in an adjacent alley, and rats scurried into holes burrowed in the lower levels of the old, dilapidated buildings.

"Christian, I don't like this," Elizabeth whispered, tugging at her husband's sleeve. "This is not an area that I want my children to spend the night."

Christian nodded, calling, "Young man, where are we going?"

"Not much further," he retorted, quickly.

However, Christian stopped as did the rest of the family. "We're not going on. Elizabeth is right. This is not a good area. Let's get out of here."

The boy continued on, not even realizing he had lost his followers as he stepped over a filthy man lying in a drunken stupor and turned into a still darker alleyway, leading to the right.

The parents hustled the children back down the alley, all relieved when they returned to a lighted street. Although turned around and lost, they sighed relief that they were safely out of the slums of Bremen, filled with drunks and god-knows-what-kind-of people.

With the children terrified and crying, the ladies did their best to soothe and quiet them, but, truthfully, the mothers were near hysteria themselves. It took every ounce of Elizabeth's strength not to bellow, "Let's go home, Christian."

The petrified look in her eyes told the story, and putting his arm around his wife, Christian said, "Come on. Let's find a safe place for you ladies and children. Conrad and I will search for rooms alone."

Fourteen tired and anxious travelers walked in the direction from which they thought they had come, searching for a café where the children could get some milk and the ladies could calm their nerves. Lena, who was a natural with youngsters, was clapping her hands to the tune of *Tanz, Kindchen, Tanz*. Eager to join in the song with Aunt Lena, they forgot the fears of the moment.

A corner café two blocks down the street provided a haven for the family, and long tables with benches and a scent of chicken soup reminded them of home. The children had found contentment for the moment, and Conrad and Christian disappeared out the door.

The ladies talked of everything except the most recent horrifying incident. For fear of bursting into tears or crying for the security and safety of their homes in Hummersen, they recited much loved nursery rhymes, one after another — "Hanschein Klein," then "Hoppe hoppe Rieter," and finally "Hansel and Gretel." Meanwhile, Regina went to a corner of the room to nurse baby Maria, who had been feeling the tension and emotional turmoil of her mother. Crying relentlessly for half an hour, she was now asleep at her mother's breast.

With a quiet moment in the corner, Regina now tried to understand exactly what had happened in the alleyways of Bremen. Was the boy leading them into a trap so that someone could steal their money? Maybe a poverty-stricken owner was giving the young boy a few schillings to bring emigrants to his filthy rooming house. What if someone had wanted the children for…. Regina closed her mind on unthinkable thoughts as she watched little Maria suckle contentedly in her sleep.

* * * * *

Within an hour, Christian and Conrad reappeared. Having walked down first one street and then another, they searched half a dozen hotels and rooming houses only to find either there was no vacancy or the rooms didn't rise to the standards of cleanliness to which the Pollmann and Haas families were accustomed. Finally, a small rooming house on a side street advertised vacancies, and as Christian and Conrad entered, they were greeted by a short, stocky German lady with sparkling green eyes and a whimsical smile. Christian immediately liked her, and the rooms met qualifications of price and cleanliness. Christian had assumed that all Germans were clean and tidy, but never having been in any homes outside of Hummersen, he was now learning quickly that such was not a shared custom everywhere. However, Frau Hoffmann's home was perfect — one that even his meticulous mother would have approved.

The owner of the cafe had been throwing the families dubious looks. Since they had been there for an hour and had ordered only milk, they were apparently taking up wanted space in the small restaurant. Happy to leave, the children quickly picked up their bundles and crowded to the door. Temporarily, they had rooms to call "home" if only for a few days.

Immediately, the families settled in. The large, spacious rooms were on the second floor, overlooking the street. Beds covered with warm, soft blankets and large feather pillows were an inviting sight for the weary travelers. On the main floor was the living and dining area, and enveloping the dining room was a huge oval oak table. As the dinner hour approached, the hungry children scurried into the room to feast on German sausage and potato salad. Frau Hoffmann — now dressed in a tidy, lace-trimmed, flowered apron and pale pink dust cap — bustled about, juggling the serving spoons, bowls, and trays.

With laughter and nonstop chatter, it was entertainment that all of them needed this first night in a dauntingly strange city, and Frau's eyes glistened as she watched the children heap their plates. Ravenous after a long day of frustration, the families savored each bite as if they were being served rare delicacies.

"Frau Hoffmann, do you have children?" Lena ventured to ask.

"Oh, my, yes. I have four children and thirteen grandchildren. Most live in the area and Hans and Martin — my two oldest grandsons — help me out here at the rooming house. In fact, they'll help you tomorrow when you get tickets."

Christian smiled. "That would be wonderful because my next question was going to be where we should buy tickets."

"That problem will be taken care of — tomorrow," she grinned again, the whimsical look reappearing on her face.

Frau must have been in her seventies, Christian thought, but her vigor and love of life showed through her shining, green eyes, and suddenly he realized that Frau reminded him of his Oma Elisabetha Pollmann, his father's mother, with whom he had spent so much time as a child.

As an extended family, Heinrich's parents had lived with them in the Pollmann homestead. Oma Pollmann, a stocky German lady, had the same sparkling green eyes as Frau Hoffmann. With a hearty laugh that often bubbled to the surface, Oma's love of life showed in every aspect of daily living. With children always at her knees and tugging on her apron, she loved to coddle and play with them, ignoring household tasks until the youngsters were tucked into bed. Long into the night, Oma would bake, clean, and mend, harboring an inexhaustible amount of energy.

She taught Christian the love of nature as the two would sometimes sneak off in the evenings to saunter along the ice cold brook which originated in the mountains miles away and then meandered through the grassy Prussian valley. They'd sit and watch the pinks and oranges streak through the sky as the sun would begin its descent on the western horizon. Oma shared stories with Christian of olden times in the Bavarian capital city of Munich where she had been raised. She talked of her carefree childhood days as she and her sisters would take a basket lunch, mount their horses, and picnic in the nearby hills. Coming from a well-to-do family, she experienced all the luxuries of nice clothes, fine food, and parties.

It was at one of these social gatherings one spring evening in 1799 that she met Johann Pollmann. Having come to the party with an acquaintance, Johann did not belong to the high society and was awestruck not only with the opulent, glittering decorations, but also with Elisabetha Kiel, adorn in a pale green gown that matched her eyes. Because of his natural charisma and charming smile, Elisabetha was intrigued with Johann Pollmann. There was a kind of magic in his personality and a definite chemistry in their relationship. Despite the threats of disinheritance from her father, Elisabetha left home to marry Johann, never looking back at her lost social status.

"Christian," Elizabeth's voice pulled him from his dream. "Shall we go to our room? The children are tired."

"Yes, of course, dear," he answered, rising to help Elizabeth from her chair. Always very much the gentleman, Christian never forgot his father's strict rule of treating every woman with respect and courtesy.

"Thank you, Frau Hoffmann. The meal was delicious," Regina commented. "We appreciate your hospitality."

"More than you'll ever know," Louisa inserted.

Saying their goodnights, the weary travelers climbed the stairs to their rooms, glad that the first day was behind them but leery of what might possibly be ahead.

Twelve

TICKETS TO AMERICA

Christian and Conrad didn't look forward to going out into the mass of people the next morning in search of thirteen tickets — baby Maria would go free. By 8 o'clock, they were all sitting together at Frau Hoffmann's dining table eating boiled eggs, cheese, bread, and drinking coffee as they waited for Hans and Martin to appear. Frau's grandsons would be a welcome addition not only in searching for tickets but also in getting through the astounding number of people in Bremen.

Near 9 o'clock, two young lads appeared — Martin was ten, fragile with dark hair and eyes. Hans, a cousin, was older — perhaps thirteen — stocky built with the typical German blonde hair, blue eyes. Eager to help get tickets for the Pollmanns, they declined their grandmother's breakfast invitation, and as the gentlemen hurriedly took their last sips of coffee, they folded their napkins, thanked Frau Hoffmann, and started out the door, the boys leading the way.

The walk was short to the docks, and the young lads chattered incessantly to Chris and Conrad, and the two men asked various questions concerning the industries in Bremen and transportation to Bremerhaven. The boys seemed knowledgeable and had been working for their grandmother intermittently for several years, as they tried to attend half-day school plus earn money to help their families.

It was on Wasser Strasse, a wide boulevard directly across from the docks, that a large foreboding building stood with numerous windows and an elegant façade. At street level, a door was wedged open, and already a line of people was extended outward into the street. All shabbily dressed people, the motley group were all attempting to get inside. With rucksacks on their backs, most clung to equally poorly dressed children. An air of intense silent agitation permeated the crowd as they waited.

A sign "Bremerhaven Shipping Agents" hung above the partially open door as Hans pointed towards it.

"There it is. The tickets for the steerage section of the ships is always long so we may as well get at the back of the line. It moves fairly quickly. Either the passenger has the money or he doesn't," Hans concluded in an adult-like fashion.

Several well-dressed gentlemen approached an officially dressed constable and were hurried inside through a side door.

Hans noticed Christian watching and whispered, "First-class passengers. They get priority service."

Christian nodded.

With such a large crowd, the people were remarkably controlled. Only once did the constable have to break up an unruly man from harassing another passenger, and, in general, Hans was right — the line moved fairly quickly. In three hours, Conrad and Christian were close enough to read the small lettering on the sign in the window — "Tickets Steerage." A placard listed two-weeks' dates of departure, destinations, and ship names. As people neared the window, they became more agitated as they consulted the placard, their friends, relatives, and purses.

Christian and Conrad had been warned back in Hummersen to put their money in a safe place since hundreds of people were robbed before they ever got to the purchasing window. Christian had a pouch tied around the calf of his leg, the money well hidden by his trousers and boots. He felt now was the time to retrieve it since they were minutes away from buying tickets, and he bent to raise his pant's leg and undo the pouch's string. Cautiously, he put the pouch in his hand, grasping it firmly.

When it was their turn, it seemed almost all too easy. A ship would leave in two days, going to New Orleans. The tickets cost 100 Talers for adults and 50 for children under twelve years of age — perfect. The clerk quickly counted the tickets and handed them to Conrad as Christian sorted through the money. Carefully counting the tickets, Conrad immediately realized that there were seven children's tickets but only five adult.

"Sir, excuse me, but we need six adult tickets," Conrad told the clerk.

"There are six there," the clerk retorted. "I counted them myself."

"No, sir, there are five," Conrad said, laying the tickets on the counter in full view of the clerk.

"You've hidden one" was the quick reply. "Don't try to cheat me. The constable is right over there. I gave you six, you scoundrel."

An argument pursued with the clerk insisting the two men had been dishonest. No need for the Frau's grandsons to act as alibis — they were too young plus the clerk was in charge and the "constables" were present. Christian and Conrad knew that they mustn't create a scene or they could be arrested and so they yielded.

Silently, Christian was grateful that Conrad had counted the tickets. What if they had gotten to the boat, short one ticket? He didn't even want to think of that.

Now, however, the clerk had no more adult tickets for that departure — the ship was sold out. The next possible boat would be in four days for which they could purchase six adult and seven children's tickets, but the men were forced to pay for the ticket that they had "stolen." Regrettably, Christian counted money for six adult and seven children's tickets — fortunately, baby Maria went free. The departure date was set for March 16 on the *Don Quixote*.

Holding tightly to the tickets, the men and two boys quickly left the ticket window and scrambled down an alley. Being alone and unseen was imperative as Christian took the tickets and handed them to Conrad. Regina had sewn an inside pocket on the band of Conrad's trousers to keep the tickets safe. If Christian had carried the money, it was better now for Conrad to hide the tickets. The pouch that had been tied to Christian's leg was not the best place for the tickets as some travelers had seen him retrieve the money from it. Since the clerk had been crafty, the Hummersen men now knew that there were crooks on every corner in the big city. All measures to dissuade thievery had to be employed.

"How did you happen to have 100 extra Talers?" Conrad questioned as he glanced at the tickets still clutched in his hand.

"I had saved extra money, wanting to buy Elizabeth dress material for new clothes once we got to America. I'm afraid her old clothes will…"

He never finished the sentence as Conrad interrupted with "Oh, no."

"What, Conrad?"

"These tickets are from Bremerhaven to New York City. We wanted New Orleans." Agitation as well as fear sounded in Conrad's voice as Christian took the tickets, scrutinizing them quickly.

"We need to talk to the clerk immediately," Conrad said.

All the while the two boys had been silent, but Hans spoke up now. "Don't go back out there with the tickets. First, you'll have to wait in line again. No one will let you at the front to exchange anything. Second, you chance having someone swipe the tickets from you while waiting in line again. People have seen you get tickets."

Although Hans was only thirteen, he spoke with wisdom beyond his years. Because he had helped many people rooming at his grandmother's, he had seen thievery every day.

"Besides," little Martin chimed in, "Even if you still have your tickets by the time you get to the front of the line, you'll never get that many again for a boat going this week. You'll be staying five or six days longer in Bremen."

"What about asking the constable to help?" Conrad questioned. The phrase was hardly from his mouth when he realized the folly of it. The constable was present for "looks," and probably he took whatever bribes were offered by clerks or passengers.

Conrad's question was left unanswered as Christian commented," I think that the boys are right on all points, Conrad. I see why your grandmother sent you boys along," he said, ruffling Martin's hair as the boys beamed. "Going up the Mississippi River to Missouri would have been easy, but that plan is not feasible now. Once we're in New York City, we'll just have to figure out how to get to Illinois. Maybe others on the boat will have ideas. At least we'll be in America." Another thought entered into Christian's mind. "And our trunks are being sent to New York City. Maybe we can pick them up before we head for the Midwest, and we won't have to wait for a month to get them. That would be a great piece of luck," Chris said with a smile.

Conrad nodded. Checking that no one was watching, he carefully deposited the tickets into the inside pocket, and the two boys led them from the center of town through the back alleyways to their grandmother's rooming house.

"We're going to take the long way," Hans commented. "We don't want to go back into that crowd because you have tickets. Even though these alleys don't look safe, they're better than the main streets where people have already seen your faces and know that you have precious tickets to America. You can't trust anyone."

Again, Christian was grateful that they had been fortunate enough to find Frau Hoffmann and her grandsons. Hustling through the same garbage-filled, filthy alleys that they had trod the day before, the four dodged drunks, who were looking for booze to get them through the day. After tramping through numerous alleys, the third one opened onto a wide boulevard, and Christian recognized it as the one leading to the rooming house. With an audible sigh of relief, he felt his muscles relax.

At the first sight of Frau Hoffmann's house, Christian could see the children's faces plastered against the upstairs window and hear their excited shouts. In a brief moment, the ladies appeared at the window, too, and Conrad and Christian beamed and waved, a sure sign that they had been successful in their pursuit of tickets.

Thirteen

MEDICAL EXAMS

The story of the tickets was guarded from the children. They were simply told that there was a little trouble and not all people are honest.

"How could someone not be truthful?" little Karl asked. "I thought everyone was honest."

"Not so, son," Louisa replied. "We're not in Hummersen now. We all must be a little leery."

"Are they honest in America?" he asked with an innocent, wide-eyed stare.

"Once we're out of the big cities, I think that there'll be less to worry about," Christian inserted. "Dishonest people sometimes live in big places like Bremen. New York City will be very large so we'll have to be careful there, too, so just hold tight to one of our hands. Soon we'll be in Illinois with your pa, and all will be safe."

Karl's eyes beamed at the mention of his father as he looked at his mother for reassurance. Louisa nodded as she squeezed his small hand.

With the task of buying tickets completed, Frau Hoffmann suggested that the group go for their medical exams first thing in the morning.

"Medical exams? What do you mean?" Conrad asked, perplexed.

"Oh, you must have a governmental medical exam before boarding the ship," Frau answered.

"We didn't know that," Conrad replied. "Where do we get such an exam?"

"Don't worry. The boys will take you," Frau replied. "I'm told that it's not usually a problem. You stick out your tongue, and they say 'you're fine,'" Frau grinned.

"So everyone must have one?" Christian asked.

"Yes, even the baby," she answered.

Amazed that no one at the ticket booth had mentioned a medical exam, Christian realized it was possibly done on purpose. Many people paid for a ticket and then didn't get to use it because they didn't have an exam. The ship could then resell the ticket and make money. Yes, there were truly crooked people everywhere, waiting for an opportunity to cheat an innocent person out of his money, thought Christian. Again thankful that they were staying with Frau Hoffmann because of the most recent information that they wouldn't have known, the Pollmanns relaxed near the fire, spending the afternoon reading and playing games.

That evening, friends of Frau Hoffmann came over with an accordion and harmonica. Frau claimed that they often dropped by to lighten the evening of travelers who were sometimes anxious about their upcoming trip.

Singing some of the old German folk songs — *Lovely is the World, If the Spring is Nigh, and Now Comes the Merry Summertime* — the Pollmanns sang and danced until far past the children's bedtime. It was the type of evening they needed, though, and it was wonderful to see the children laugh till they cried joyful tears.

"Mama, will we be this happy in America?" Anna-Marie asked her mother as they all got ready for bed.

"Of course, darling. Pa has it all planned for us, and once we find Uncle Fredrich, all will be fine. We'll have a nice home in Illinois. Don't worry about anything, my sweet girl," replied Elizabeth, reassurance sounding in her voice, but in her heart, she still felt intermittent anxiety.

The children were all nestled three to a bed or in pallets on the floor. The adults sat and talked far into the night about their day of departure — March 16 — the frightening voyage, and the new unexpected journey from New York City to Illinois. Long after midnight, Christian and Elizabeth got into bed. Unbeknownst to Chris, Elizabeth felt ill and wished she had one of her mother's poultices for her head, which was throbbing relentlessly.

* * * * *

By 9 o'clock in the morning, Hans and Martin appeared to take the families for medical exams. Everyone but Elizabeth was in the living room, having finished breakfast by 8 o'clock. Christian was finishing a third cup of coffee when Elizabeth called from upstairs.

"Come on, Elizabeth. We're ready to go," Chris said as he climbed the stars.

"I'm ill, Chris," she said, her hands shaking slightly. Her headache continued as she sat on the edge of the bed.

"What's wrong, darling?"

"I felt faint after breakfast, and as I started to lie down for a moment, I vomited."

"I'll send the others ahead, and we'll go later for the exam," Chris suggested.

"No, no, I'll be fine. Let me lie here a moment. See if Frau has a cup of tea."

Within half an hour, Elizabeth had convinced her husband that she was better, and they all left the house as Hans and Martin led, and they headed for a small street not far from Wasser Strasse where they had purchased tickets the previous day.

Hemmed in on both sides by stone buildings that were plastered with signs depicting dates and names of departing ships — *Mercury* departing to New Orleans on 13 March; *John Harward* departing to New York City on 14 March; *Don Quixote* departing to New York City on 16 March.

"There's our ship," Conrad said, pointing to the sign, and little Karl clapped, showing the excitement for all.

A dingy, gray building at the far end of the street held a placard saying "Governmental Medical Exams held between 9.00 and 17.00 hours."

The small street was crammed with emigrants, and a long line at the door to the medical office ensued. Christian noted to Conrad that no constable was present. They weren't, however, sure that it would have made a difference.

"Will the line move quickly?" Conrad asked the boys as all took their places at the end.

"It'll move fairly fast because the exams are brief," Martin answered.

It was a challenge, however, this time as the children were in line as well, and after the first hour, they became restless.

"What if Louisa and I take the children for a walk?" Lena suggested.

Hans shook his head. "No, Lena, you mustn't. First, it's not safe for you ladies to be alone with the children on the streets, and second, people won't let you back in line. They are cruel when it comes to cutting in front even though someone is saving your place."

"You're kidding, of course," Lena commented.

"No, he's serious," Martin replied. "We saw quite a raucous last week when a father took his children for food. Fortunately, a constable was present, and he let the father back in line. People were crazy."

A middle-aged gentleman behind the Pollmanns tapped Chris on the shoulder and whispered, "You go ahead and take the children for a walk. We'll let you back in."

Christian looked a big dubious. "Thank you, but I guess we can't be sure that the people behind you will also be compliant."

"Yes, please, go ahead," replied the young man who was further back in line. "It's cruel to keep children tied down for hours."

Thanking them, Lena, Regina, and Christian took the children by their hands, giving the youngsters a reprieve by walking with them to the river to watch the boats sailing toward Bremerhaven. People on the departing boats waved their goodbyes to families and friends as they went toward their ships in Bremerhaven, which would soon leave for the New World.

By early afternoon, the Pollmanns were close enough to the door of the examining room that they could hear the conversations inside.

"Ticket?" they heard the examiner ask. "All right. Now, stick out your tongue. Are you well?" The answer was inaudible, but it must have been affirmative, and his tongue must have passed inspection as the official then said "move on" as he stamped the ticket.

As the Pollmanns stepped into the large, bare room, a small table sat at one end. The medical examiner, red-faced and bald with rimmed glasses perched on his nose, was the only official visible. He looked disheveled after a morning of monotonous "exams," and as the Pollmanns entered, a new examiner came onto the scene. Obviously, it was a change of shifts.

The new examiner pushed several people through quickly, and then abruptly retained a young couple as he questioned them about their tickets. The two were obviously agitated — Chris couldn't hear the conversation — and the young lady was weeping as her husband pounded his fist on the table. The examiner yelled for an officer, who appeared out of nowhere and escorted the young couple from the premises. The crowd was stunted into silence, and word quickly spread to the other passengers outside that someone had been denied.

Tension followed as the crowd tried to watch the examiner's facial expressions as his fat, pockmarked face was frequently skewed into distorted smirks. As Louisa and her three children approached him, the examiner looked at the tickets, mumbled something to her, stamped them, and waved them on. The rest of the family relaxed a bit as the official seemed barely concerned with Louisa's family. As Christian, Elizabeth, and the girls approached, he glanced at the tickets, asked if they were well, stamped the tickets, and motioned the Pollmanns through. Christian audibly sighed in relief.

Regina and Conrad were last, and as Christian started out the back door, he turned to see the examiner looking at the baby, Maria. Shaking his head, the official pointed to the door through which they had come. and dejectedly — with fear showing in his eyes — Conrad looked at Christian who had stopped dead in astonishment.

"Conrad and Regina are turning back," Chris said to Elizabeth, who was ahead of him with the children. A look of apprehension crossed her face as she turned to look at her husband. "They're returning to the front of the building," Christian said as they all pushed through the crowd to round the building in search of their rejected family members.

Searching the crowd of emigrants, Christian saw the back of Conrad's head in the throng of people at the front of the medical building. Pushing towards him was no easy task. Regina was crying when Christian and Elizabeth finally got within earshot.

"He said Maria has a rash and won't let her board the ship," Regina cried. "I tried to explain that it's heat rash from being wrapped too warmly in blankets, but the examiner insisted it was small pox."

"Look, Regina," Elizabeth said, trying to remain calm as she examined the few small red pimples. "They'll be gone in a day if you uncover Maria a bit so that the air can reach her skin. You and Conrad can return then."

Regina, trying to stifle her sobs, looked at Conrad who nodded. "Yes, it'll be fine, Regina. Let's go back to Frau Hoffmann's and give Maria a cool bath. Wrap her lightly the rest of the day."

"Can't we go to America?" cried little Christoph, confused about the entire situation as he clung to his father's hand.

"Yes, of course, darling, we'll get to go," answered Regina. "We'll just have to come back here tomorrow."

The group was somber as they walked the cobblestone streets back to the rooming house. Elizabeth seemed tired, lagging behind, and because of the morning episode, Christian worried that she had contracted an illness. Insisting she was fine, Elizabeth picked up Anna-Marie who was dragging her feet. Chris lifted Margaretha into one arm and Karl into the other. Even through neither had complained, he knew the four-year-olds had to be tired. Together they all reached the rooming house and retold the story to Frau Hoffmann.

"Not to worry, Regina," Frau reassured her. "Put it into God's hands. Maria will pass the test. Come, we'll fill the wash tub with lukewarm water."

By evening, Maria's rash was gone, and Conrad and Regina were anticipating another morning of long lines leading to the medical examiner. Elizabeth had retired early, and Christian had said an extra prayer for her as a silent fear tightened in his stomach.

Fourteen

READY TO SAIL

The morning dawned overcast with the threat of rain. Bundled against the possible threat of storms, Conrad, Regina, and the children waited for Hans and Martin to take them back to the medical examiner. Chris debated whether to follow his brother-in-law and family, but when Elizabeth vomited her breakfast, his mind was made up. He stayed with his wife who seldom was ill with even a slight headache. Already suspicious about her illness, Elizabeth refrained from lying down this time, saying it was nothing, and she was feeling better.

"How can you be okay when you're vomiting? Maybe you've become run down with all the preparation and work for the trip, or maybe you caught the flu," Chris surmised.

"I don't think so, Chris."

"What then?"

Hesitantly, she replied, "I think maybe I'm pregnant."

With everything else going on, that thought was the furthest from Christian's mind. Unable to answer, he stared at his wife until he finally mouthed, "Really?"

"Well, I'm not certain, but I'm never ill. My other pregnancies have all started with morning sickness and unusual tiredness in the evening. I've experienced both of these for two weeks."

"You didn't say anything until yesterday," Chris replied.

"Well, I had hoped I was wrong. We want another child, but the timing isn't good right now."

Chris smiled. "Another child is welcome at anytime, Elizabeth, but I'll worry about your health on the ship."

"I'll be fine, Chris," she said, squeezing his hand. "Let's see if Lena will watch the girls, and we can take a walk. The fresh air will do me good."

* * * * *

By 11 o'clock, Chris and Elizabeth were just returning from a stroll along the river. The two had walked hand-in-hand, remembering the birth of their firstborn. Margaretha had come three weeks early and much faster than the midwife had ever expected. After only two hours of labor, Elizabeth — along with Christian's help — delivered a 7 pound, 3 ounce baby girl. It was a joyous time, and even though the two had little money, it hadn't mattered. Two years later, Anna-Marie — an 8 pound, 3 ounce baby — was born, this time with the help of the neighboring midwife.

As Elizabeth and Christian ascended the stairs to the hotel, a light mist had started although the most threatening clouds had passed. With no sign of Conrad and his family, the rest of the Pollmanns decided to spend the day near the fire, playing games and telling stories.

By 3 o'clock with no sign of Regina and Conrad, Christian had decided to go to the medical building when the door opened, letting in the wet, weary family. Hans and Martin had left them at 1 o'clock to attend their half day of school, and with an extra long line, Conrad, Regina, and the children had to wait until 2:30 to see the official. Waving them through the line, the medical examiner gave them no trouble, and baby Maria passed the test without a second glance. Conrad was relieved after a tense five hours in line.

Concerned about Regina and the children all in wet clothes, Conrad helped them get dried off as Frau served hot chocolate and soup. With the tickets stamped, and everyone departing together on March 16, Conrad finally relaxed. Carefully, he stripped off his damp shirt and laid it to dry by the fire. Christoph and Gustov — having braved the examination venture a second time — now sat together on the hearth, whimpering. Having left their beloved puppy behind with Grandpa Pollmann, they cried for Gert, their black, short-haired mutt. Undoubtedly, Gert wondered where they were as she often sat at the window in the late afternoon, waiting faithfully for Conrad to return from the field.

"We'll get a puppy when we get to Illinois," Conrad promised the boys for the um-teenth time. "Grandpa loves Gert, and she's got a fine home, and Grandpa won't be lonesome now because Gert will be his best friend," Conrad grinned.

"Do you think so?" Christoph asked.

"Yes. Grandpa needs a best friend now with Grandma gone so you guys have done him a big favor by giving him Gert," Conrad concluded.

"Will we really get a puppy, Pa?" little Gustov asked, trying to put on a brave front and fight back the tears.

"I promise. As soon as we are settled and have a little money, you boys can have a puppy," Conrad replied.

"What color do you want?" asked Regina, who also missed Gert's playful disposition.

"Black, just like Gert," said Gustov.

"And with white paws," Christoph inserted.

"Well, we'll see what we can do," Conrad said, throwing his wife a quick wink.

Afternoon faded into evening and after a warm dinner of roasted pork and potatoes straight from the fire, the family retreated to their rooms. Alone at last, Christian and Elizabeth quietly discussed the prospect of another child — the blessings as well as the consequences. With blessings definitely outweighing any repercussions, the two welcomed the thought of a new little Pollmann but decided to wait to make an announcement until they were certain.

Christian had heard dreadful stories of seasickness — even among the strong, hearty men — and his silent worry was how Elizabeth would cope. Somehow she must have known his concern because she took Christian's hand, pressing it to her lips.

"It'll be okay, Chris. Don't worry about the voyage. God is in control."

Chris was silent for a few minutes, and when he finally leaned over to kiss his wife, her steady breathing told him that she was already asleep.

Fifteen

BREMERHAVEN

On the morning of March 16, the Pollmanns were at the dock at 8 o'clock, ready to catch the boat from Bremen on the way to Bremerhaven. Just 50 kilometers south of Bremerhaven, Bremen was connected to the larger city by the Weser River, which flowed into the North Sea. Daily, dozens of boats took Germans to the harbor where they'd board their ship sailing to America.

The Pollmanns occupied two boats on their voyage to Bremerhaven. Floating on the Weser through the lush pastureland, thick forests, and mountains of northern Germany, the adults knew that they were getting their last glimpses of their fatherland. Filled with mixed emotions, Christian attempted to chat and tease with the children to occupy his mind, retracting his thoughts from the impending departure.

Bremerhaven was even more intimidating than Bremen. The small boats coming from Bremen were dwarfed by the dozens of ocean-going ships, all docked in the enormous seafaring harbor. Huge gray sails bulked large into the blue skies, which were filled with squawking seagulls flying in from the open waters. The Pollmanns all breathed deeply of the rich sea air as they scanned the horizon, trying to imagine which three-mast ship was the *Don Quixote*.

With the dock crammed with people from all over Germany, as well as other European countries, the Pollmanns scrambled to buy food at the open air markets before finding and boarding their ship. Meals — although not especially tasty — would be included, but they had been advised to buy supplies for the first day. Christian had seen a sign posted in Bremen that all passengers of the steerage class would have ample rations of rye and barley loaves, a round of cheese, 30 pounds of potatoes or rice, and a keg of butter and honey. In addition, salted pork, sausage, or mutton would be provided daily to each passenger. In limited amounts would be dried fruits and vegetables, and milk would be distributed four or five times a week to the children.

After purchasing some meager supplies, the Pollmanns went in search of a placard listing the ships and their docking number.

"Karl, do not let loose of your sisters' hands," Louisa chided her son who was looking in awe at the harbor sights. "If one of you children gets lost, we may never find you."

Chris quickly scooped Karl into his arm, never once releasing his grip on Anna-Marie. Methodically, the 14 travelers made their way through the chaos toward Dock #14 where the *Don Quixote* awaited her passengers.

As the Pollmanns reached their dock, a raucous had broken out aboard the *Fritz Johannes*, the neighboring ship. A man had attempted to leap aboard the *Fritz Johannes* near the stern. Sailors armed with long clubs rushed to the railing to meet the man, and as he reached the bulwark, a fierce struggle erupted. The sailors, outnumbering the intruder six to one, easily managed to throw him overboard. Meanwhile, the emigrants on the quay — who had been pushing to get aboard — stood frozen as they focused on the drama being played out before them. With the disturbance quelled, the surge toward the gangplank resumed.

Wide-eyed, the Pollmann children had looked questionably at the chaotic scene.

"He didn't have a ticket," Christian commented. "He was desperate to go to America, but he probably didn't have money to buy passage. Come, let's get aboard." His voice was calm, but Christian's insides were taut as they all moved toward the gangplank.

It seemed that progression was painfully slow, and then Conrad noticed that ship officers were checking tickets at the base of the ship as well as at the top of the gangway. Again searching for stowaways, they were being doubly careful that everyone aboard had paid for a ticket.

Elizabeth eyed the ship's first-mate, who was checking each passenger. Of medium build, he had massive hands, hard eyes, and a fixed scowl on his face. As if he were not imposing enough, a burly sailor stood next to him, entering names into a ledger. Elizabeth glanced at Chris who was trying to occupy the children and keep their minds off the all-too-frightening situation.

Quickly, however, all eyes were turned towards the rear of the line as a voice was heard. "Make way for a gentleman. Please, move. Gentleman boarding."

Being officially escorted to the gangplank was a well-dressed man in a black suit and hat. Obviously a first-class passenger, he was not expected to wait in line with the steerage class. Reveling at being the center of attention, the man walked grandly past the common people, and proceeded toward the gangplank. Flashing his ticket briefly at the first-mate — whose stern face softened momentarily — he was saluted and escorted by two officers up the plank and onto the bulwark.

Almost at the same moment, the passengers' attention was drawn to the top of the gangplank where a man had been turned away and was roughly being escorted down to the quay. He had not had a medical exam, and although he loudly protested, it was to no avail. The two sailors carried him down the ramp, flinging him onto the wharf amid the stunned crowd of ongoing passengers.

It was too much for little Anna-Marie, who buried her face in her father's arms and sobbed. A chain reaction ensued as Gustov, Christoph, Elise, and Margaretha all followed suit. The older children — although not crying — seemed terrified and clung tightly to their parents' hands. Overwhelmed themselves, the adults tried to soothe the children as they inched their way toward the impending first-mate.

And now as hundreds of people waited, hawkers seemed to appear out of nowhere, pushing and crowding between the weary travelers. Crying out dire predictions as to what might happen if the passengers didn't purchase food, blankets, and medicine, they shoved their supplies at each person. Several people pulled out money to buy a few items, but most travelers seemed to be aware that hawkers would attempt their scare tactics and motioned them away.

At last the Pollmanns stood in front of the first-mate. His large hands reached out for the tickets, and his cold eyes surveyed the 14 passengers as he asked for names, ages, occupations, and birthplaces of each person. The burly sailor quickly scribbled in the ledger as the first-mate checked medical exams. Within fifteen minutes, the Pollmanns were headed up the gangplank to be briefly checked a second time.

No more had they reached the deck of the ship when they heard the gangplank being taken up.

"What's happening?" Lena cried. She had brought up the rear of the 14 Pollmanns, and only six more travelers had gotten on board when the plank had been closed.

There were still thirty people standing on the quay, in line for the *Don Quixote*. Cries and screams were being wailed but to no avail. The crew had closed the ship, saying the maximum capacity of 250 passengers was aboard. The remaining people were out of luck and must trade their tickets for another ship, probably leaving on a different day. The look of horror on Lena's face told the story for all of the Pollmanns. Part of their family could have been standing down there on the quay.

Christian said his first silent prayer on board the *Don Quixote*. "Thank you, Lord, that you saw us all safely aboard the ship. Be with the crew as they guide the ship, and bless us as we journey to our new life in America."

Sixteen

THE FIRST DAY ON THE *DON QUIXOTE*

Within a few minutes, the first-mate accompanied by the burly sailor took their places upon the rail. The first-mate's façade had not changed — stern and cold — and in his huge hand was the ledger.

"I have here all the passengers who have paid. When I call your name, step forward. You'll receive your berth number. Don't forget it because it won't be repeated. Go down those steps," he said, pointing to his left, "and wait below. Anyone whose name isn't called will be removed from the ship." With his gruff look turning to a scowl, he added, "No questions asked."

Without further ado, the officer began the roll call. "Weghorst, Fredrich, wife, 2 children — berths 1, 2, and 3. Shoemaker, Adolph, wife — berths 4 and 5...."

It was a slow procedure — 250 passengers — and the Pollmanns were nearly last to be called.

"Pollmann, Christian, wife, 2 children — berths 97, 98, and 99. Kruse, Conrad, wife, 3 children — berths 100, 101, 102, and 103. Pollmann, Louisa, 3 children — berths 104, 105, and 106. Haas, Lena — berth 48."

Lena exchanged a terrified glance with her sisters. Why Berth #48? It wasn't even close to her relatives? With no chance to protest, they all picked up their rucksacks and moved toward the steps.

Two more names were called as Christian halted before descending the stairs, and still three passengers remained whose names had not been called — one man and two women. Quickly, they produced their tickets, and with tears, they protested loudly that they had paid. However, sailors appeared, grabbing a hold of the begging, rejected passengers, and forcibly took them from the ship, pushing them toward the wharf. Christian said his second silent prayers as he wondered how this could be happening. He descended the stairs.

Deciding to keep the most recent incident to himself, Chris focused on Lena's predicament. Fighting tears and trying to be brave, she talked softly with her sisters.

"Lena, you're not going to Berth #48," Conrad was insisting. "There'll be room with us."

"Maybe if I ask the first-mate. Perhaps he just made a mistake," Lena replied.

With the incident above board still fresh in his mind, Christian protested. "No, Lena, let's not. There are three sections to the ship — families, single women, and single men. You're obviously put into the single-women section. You stay with us, and no one has to know. Now, let's find our berths."

With that settled, the 14 Pollmanns went in search of their rooming assignments. If the situation seemed confused above aboard, it was utter disorder and chaos below. With 200-plus individuals crowded into the dim passages of the steerage, tempers grew thin as all clamorously inquired in various tongues about their berths. The steward, however, actually seemed somewhat friendly and in control of the situation. Seeming to understand both German and French, he pointed the passengers in the direction of their berths.

Conrad was the first to find the berths, and as the rest scrambled in his direction, they all located their compartment, small to say the least. The only standing room in each berthing area was a space of three feet wide. Rising upward were three tiers of bunks. With twenty of them in one compartment, the Pollmanns were allotted ten — five for the children and five for the adults. Into the remaining ten berths, future occupants were busy adjusting what bedding was available for them.

Christian grabbed mattresses, pillows, and bedcovers from the ship's hallway, handing them to each of the family members as he listened to the various tongues being spoken. He judged that at best, three or four countries were represented in their one compartment.

"Look, Lena, there's plenty of room for you. The adults each have a berth and the children are either one or two to a bed. You can sleep with one of the children who has the bed to herself. It'll be fine."

Lena nodded, smiling with relief.

As Conrad helped the children arrange their bedding, the family heard a male French voice demand the location of Berth #107. Turning, Conrad saw a huge, burly Frenchman and his wife moving his way. With thoughts of this 200-kilo man occupying the space above him, Conrad glanced nervously at the boards, which would support the weight of this monstrous Frenchman. Quickly, Conrad — in a delicate pantomime — suggested that the man and his wife take the lower two beds, and he would crawl to the top berth. They smiled in agreement, and in relief, Conrad hastily transferred his bedding to the upper bed.

Meanwhile, Elizabeth — often accused of being too clean — was inspecting the bedding. It consisted of a mattress and pillow — filled with straw rather than down feathers — and a blanket, all of which was questionably clean by Elizabeth's standards. With the mattresses and pillows covered in coarse canvas and the blankets differing in weight, size, and material, the bedding was not what the Haas sisters would have had in their homes. Christian had been warned in advance that wearing your clothing at night was normally necessary in order to stay warm. After scrutinizing his lightweight blanket, he was convinced that no one in steerage class would undress for bed. Already cool in the early afternoon, the room would, undoubtedly, be cold on the open sea at night.

As Elizabeth and Christian examined their bedding, Conrad was searching for extra space to place his hand luggage. Each berth, six feet long and four feet wide, had to house all of the passengers' belongings. With no hooks to hang clothing, all extra possessions had to be kept in the rucksack or hung on the framework of the berth. In addition, towels and toiletries — which each passenger brought — had to be stored in the already crowded berth as well as eating utensils furnished by the ship.

"So this is our home for two months," Christian tried to say lightly with a grin. "We just have to remember this is not permanent."

Elizabeth nodded without answering as she tried to arrange the children's berths and rucksacks.

"We'll be fine, Uncle Chris," commented seven-year-old Mary. "You know, Pa made it, and he was all alone. At least we have each other for comfort." With the statement that contained wisdom beyond her years, Mary pulled from her rucksack a linen pillowcase with delicately embroidered red and blue flowers. In one quick motion, she covered the course canvas pillow with the beautiful linen cloth. Onto the bed, she strewn a sky-blue crocheted shawl, and the dingy berth immediately took on a comfortable, homey look.

"How did you think to bring something so lovely, Mary?" Regina asked, wishing she had had the insight to do the same.

"Pa's letters described the ship and the voyage, and I knew I'd need something special from home to look at for two months," she smiled.

* * * * *

Within an hour, everyone was above board to watch the ship's departure. Amidst a multitude of tears, laughter, singing, and prayers, the passengers waved to the people on the quay as the *Don Quixote* moved slowly out into the open North Sea. New waves of uncertainty and fear possessed many of the travelers as they faced the thoughts of a turbulent voyage and the beginnings of a new life in America.

Trees, houses, and the German shore land was still distinguishable for a time until fog and mist started to clog the sight. Christian noticed for the first time that many of the people who had crowded onto the deck were in tattered clothes. Everyone was advised to bring a new, fresh suit of clothing to wear when the ship landed in America, and the old clothes would then be thrown overboard.

As soon as the ship was out to sea, the Pollmanns went below and lay on their berths, resting after a stressful day, and already by early evening and two hours at sea, everyone was feeling the effects of the tossing brought on by each wave. Few felt like eating anything, and the children throughout the steerage area were crying relentlessly. To add to the problem, the limited space in the compartments made the air stuffy. Two 12-inch ventilator shafts were required for every 50 persons in each compartment, but the provisions seemed insufficient.

Conrad had been told by one of the shipmates that going above to the open air helped ease the seasickness, and so as the sun started to set late into the evening, the Pollmanns all made their way to the stern, watching the huge red ball cast pink, yellow, and orange streaks throughout the dusky sky.

"Red sky in morning, sailors take warning; red sky at night, sailors' delight," said Elizabeth as she looked onto the spectacular horizon, with the sun showering the sky with a multitude of colors.

"What's that mean?" Elise asked.

"If the sky is red in the morning, it's a bad sign — storms are brewing, I guess. A red sky at night means that it has been a perfect day and the weather will remain good. I heard the verse when I was a child, but it all takes on a new meaning when we're on the open sea, huh?" Elizabeth concluded.

Far into the night, the Pollmanns remained on deck, walking from the stern to the bow, watching the stars come out and breathing the fresh sea air, which seemed to relieve the initial seasickness. One by one, they finally made their way below deck, with Christian and Conrad being the last to leave the open air.

"I guess, it could be a rough journey — rougher than I thought," commented Conrad.

"We'll make it, though, Conrad. The two of us must remain strong for the women and children. I think of the lady in Detmold who went with her seven children, the twins being only seven months old, to meet her husband in Pennsylvania. If she could make this voyage alone, then we can make it together," Christian smiled. "The Lord is with us — what more could we ask?" he concluded as the two men started toward the stairs that descended into the steerage class, which already reeked of the foul smell of vomit.

Seventeen

JURGEN AND KASIMIR

As one day blurred into another, seasickness was — at first — the main concern. Christian was apprehensive about Elizabeth's health as she was deathly ill for a week. Having confided in her sisters that she thought she was pregnant, they all took turns bringing her tea and rusks, which Elizabeth seemed to be able to tolerate.

With no receptacles furnished for seasick passengers, Christian scoured the kitchen area, begging for a can. Able to trade one of his wife's lace handkerchiefs for a rusty tin can, Christian rushed back to Elizabeth before she became ill again. It was a crude receptacle, but under the circumstances, Elizabeth didn't seem to mind.

As the mornings passed into the afternoons, Elizabeth usually felt well enough to go on deck and take deep breaths of fresh air. There, she and Chris stood as long as the weather allowed. The two were on the stern the second day after they had left German soil — it was March 18. The daylight was ending as the sun started to recede under the horizon when Christian saw the towers and the chalky cliffs of England. To the right was the city of Dover and to the left — far in the distance — was France and the city of Gaulle.

Pointing them out to Elizabeth, both felt a moment of excitement as well as sadness. Never having been out of Lipperland, the Pollmanns rejoiced at seeing the sight of new lands. However, it was also a moment of melancholy as they stood watching England pass in front of their eyes, knowing that their beloved Germany was behind them, lost forever.

Some passengers spoke with anger that Germany had deserted them, forcing them to seek refuge in a foreign land, thousands of miles from home. Listening, Christian winced as he again felt pangs of guilt that he was moving his family into uncertain condition. Elizabeth felt her husband's muscles tighten at hearing the Germans express their dismay.

"Don't listen to those men, Chris," Elizabeth whispered, placing her hand on her husband's arm. "We need to be thankful that we had money for passage and that our health allowed us to travel. Those people are ungrateful and will never succeed in life."

Kissing her on the cheek, he replied, "You are my inspiration, darling. I thank God that He put you into my life."

∗ ∗ ∗ ∗ ∗

Six-year-old Elise and five-year-old Christoph had always been bonded, and being confined together in adjoining berths on the ship was the height of excitement for them — they could whisper late into the night, their parents unaware.

"Ma," Christoph said one morning. "May Elise and I go above board to play? It's dark down here."

At first Louisa and Regina were reluctant to let their two children play and explore the ship alone, but Conrad interceded. "Regina, you're being overprotective. The children can't run anywhere — they're confined to the ship. They're safe. Let them play."

Hesitant at first, the mothers finally agreed, and the two youngsters always returned just in time for lunch and supper each day, but other than that, they had one childhood adventure after another.

Elizabeth and Regina reminisced how they used to go into Hummersen on Sunday afternoons when they were little. They would play hide and seek in the streets and alleyways and then dash through the fields of coneflowers outside of town. The two would play tag until they realized it was far past suppertime, and they'd surely be reprimanded by their pa.

One night, two weeks after the ship had departed, the children had returned from their nightly trek to the washroom where their mothers had scrubbed them in the cold, salt water. The provisions in the lavatory were insufficient for the number of people using them, and floors of the washrooms and water closets were normally damp and filthy. The Haas sisters were reluctant to use the facilities, but given no choice, they yielded. The children didn't seem to notice although they had never seen filthy floors even once in their homes.

Whispering and giggling continued long after Conrad had told the children that it was bedtime. He was losing patience with his son, asking what was so interesting that it couldn't wait until morning, when Christoph let the secret slip.

"Jurgen and Kasimir have to sleep in barrels because they have no parents, and..."

Silenced with a poke in his ribs by Elise who was sitting on the edge of his bed, too late Christoph realized his folly.

"Who are Jurgen and Kasimir?" Conrad questioned, glancing at his wife who was now sitting up, wide-eyed.

Without waiting for an answer, Louisa asked, "Elise, what do you know of this?" Rising onto one elbow, she stared at her daughter.

"Well..." Elise's eyes met her mother's, and she knew she was trapped — she'd have to confess. "They're stowaways, Ma."

Quickly, Louisa looked over her shoulder, checking that no neighbors were listening. Then, placing her index finger next to her mouth, she reminded the children to talk in hushed tones so as not to attract attention.

Elise continued in a whisper, "They're orphans who have stowed away in barrels in the bowels of the ship." Her words poured out as the family sat in stunned silence.

"Orphans — staying in barrels?" Conrad finally stuttered. The two nodded. "How old are they?"

"Don't know. About our age, I guess," Christoph answered. "They ran away because they were beaten often. They came from Hanover."

"And how did they get to Bremerhaven?" Elizabeth stammered, now captivated by the unbelievable story.

"Hitched rides, saying they were heading to their uncle's farm…walked… jumped aboard locomotives," Christoph replied. "Any way they could travel, they did. They're nice boys, Ma," he said to Regina. "They're hungry and scared."

"Take me to them," Conrad said, swinging his feet unto the floor and pulling on his boots.

"You won't turn them in, will you, Pa?" Elise asked.

"No, of course not. I want to help them."

Christian and Conrad rose from their berths as the children slid their bare feet into their shoes and silently crept through the darkened steerage compartment.

✳ ✳ ✳ ✳ ✳

Making the trek into the bowels of the ship, there, in the dim, damp, rat-invested lower level, Christian and Conrad found two frightened children, stuffed into two barrels that should have contained grain. Their thin faces made their round, pale blue eyes even more pronounced, and in the dim light, it was difficult to tell if their hair was brown or simply filthy. Fear showed not only through their pale eyes, but also in the small, tense muscles of their face and neck.

"It's okay, guys. My pa and uncle want to help," Christoph said as the boys crawled from the barrels.

"How did you get here?" Conrad asked as he helped Kasimir — the smaller, frailer of the two — climb out of the wooden entrapment.

"We ran away from the orphanage," Kasimir answered, "and Guido helped us onto the boat as stowaways." Kasimir was dreadfully thin, Conrad noticed, and his frail arms consisted of nothing more than skin covering bone.

"Who is Guido?" Christian asked, as he tried to hide his amazement that two children — probably five or six years of age — could have managed on their own through the German countryside and were resourceful enough to get aboard the ship.

"We met him in Bremerhaven and became friends with him," Jurgen answered. "We were sleeping in the street below the boarding house that Guido stayed in until his ship sailed."

Jurgen seemed a little older than his companion, but he, too, was amazingly emaciated. Both had ragged haircuts, and little Kasimir had obvious bald spots where hair had either fallen out because of malnutrition or had been yanked out by a cruel caretaker. Both Christian and Conrad had heard of the inhumane conditions at some of the government-owned orphanages but didn't want to believe what they hoped were unfounded rumors. By the looks of these two orphans, all stories were valid.

"Guido has been bringing us food and water," Kasimir inserted. He resisted saying that Elise and Christoph had also brought food for fear of causing them trouble. Both adults, however, guessed that their children had been involved in supplying nutrition for the stowaways.

"You two can't stay here for the duration of the trip," Chris said as they looked with sympathy at the poor, tattered boys. "I know the officers watch for stowaways. Are they looking for you?" Christian asked.

"We don't think so," Jurgen responded. "No one has been down here anyway except for Christoph, Elise, and Guido."

"Then we need to try to sneak the boys above board and into our berths," Conrad commented, looking at Chris who nodded.

"What will Ma say?" Christoph asked.

"Your ma and aunts will readily agree. You know how they feel about children. They'll take them in as their own," Conrad replied, knowing full well the emotions of his wife and her sisters.

"We don't want you to call attention to yourselves, though, so we'll try to get clothes for you and someone will come down to bathe you and cut your hair," Conrad continued. "We'll be back as soon as we can. We'll have to be careful so we're not caught."

The two boys nodded, and Christian noticed the first glimmer of a smile from Kasimir. Jurgen remained somber, perhaps suspicious — or maybe he was older and felt the weight of responsibility for both of them upon his shoulders. At any rate, his eyes reflected the pain and struggle he had experienced in his short life.

While Christian, Elise, and Christoph stayed below, Conrad checked the stairs and the steerage area. It took ten minutes before Conrad felt it was safe for the four to emerge. Once out of the lower level, they attempted to walk nonchalantly to their berths, checking to be sure they weren't being watched.

What a story they had to tell as they entered their compartment, as ten pairs of eyes focused on the door, awaiting their return.

SUITCASES OF
EMIGRANTS IN
BREMERHAVEN BEFORE
COMING TO AMERICA

BOAT ON THE WESER RIVER

BOAT IN THE HARBOR
OF BREMERHAVEN

VIEW OF WESER RIVER LEADING TO BREMERHAVEN

SHIP RECORD OF CHRISTIAN POLLMANN COMING TO AMERICA

FLOWERS AND FARMHOUSE
NEAR HUMMERSEN

MY MOTHER, MABEL POLLMAN
HOYT, GRANDAUGHTER OF
ELIZABETH HASS POLLMANN
(ONE OF THE N'S WAS DROPPED IN
POLLMANN WHEN THEY MOVED
TO AMERICA)

SIGN TO HUMMERSEN AND
NEARBY VILLAGE

SCHWALENBERG WHERE
CHRISTIAN GOT PAPERS
TO GO TO AMERICA

THE ORIGINAL
POLLMANN HOUSE IN
HUMMERSEN

VILLAGE AND
RIVER SCENE NEAR
HUMMERSEN

ONE OF THE PICTURES THAT CHRISTIAN BROUGHT TO AMERICA— WITHOUT A HOLY CROSS, THERE IS NO CROWN

SECOND PICTURE CHRISTIAN BROUGHT FROM GERMANY— WITHOUT THE HOLY CROSS, THERE IS NO SALVATION

1800S IN PEKIN FROM *PEKIN SESQUICENTENNIAL* 1824–1974

CHRISTIAN, ELIZABETH, AND GEORGE (MY GRANDPA) STANDING IN FRONT OF THE POLLMAN HOUSE THEY BUILT IN PEKIN IN 1800S.... STILL STANDING

HARDWARE STORE IN DOWNTOWN PEKIN

EVANGELICAL AND REFORMED
CHURCH IN PEKIN....CHRISTIAN
WAS ONE OF THE FOUNDERS

POLLMAN FAMILY IN AMERICAN...
HARRY, MABEL (MY MOM), EMMA,
MINNIE, GEORGE, MY GRANDPA
GEORGE POLLMAN AND MY GRANDMA
KATHERINE, FRONT IS RUTH

MY COUSIN, EDITH, AND I IN
FRONT OF THE FALKENHAGEN
CHURCH

JAN AT THE SIGN OF
HERGERSHAUSEN WHERE
ELIZABETH WAS BORN

POLLMANN GRAVE
IN GERMANY

Eighteen

THE POLLMANNS MEET THE ORPHANS

With everyone asking questions at once, it was difficult for the four to tell their story. As Conrad expected, the ladies were in favor of bringing the orphans to stay with them. However, their fear was having "the neighbors" ask questions as to whom the boys belonged. No one must know they were stowaways for fear they'd be turned in to authorities.

"If they both stay on the top berth and lay low during the daytime hours, no one may even know they're there," suggested Elizabeth. "We can put up something to partition the top berths and block the view."

"What do you suggest, Ma?" Margaretha asked.

"May we borrow your shawl, Mary?" Elizabeth asked, looking at her niece.

"Of course," she answered, already handing it to Elizabeth.

"I have something, too," Margaretha cried, her eyes lighting with a thought. "I have Emma's blanket. She'll be fine without it. I'll keep her warm." The doll's blanket was immediately shed for the purpose of a partition as Margaretha beamed.

"Thank you, sweetheart. That'll be perfect," Elizabeth responded.

For the next hour, plans were formulated in hushed tones, and Conrad suggested that he'd lead the way for Lena — the family's best barber — so she could sneak first to the stern and then down the hatchway to the lower level.

With the cover of darkness at midnight, the two silently slipped to the stern, surveying the stairs carefully from a corner where they could remain unseen. There seemed to be no dogwatch — sailors on the lookout — and feeling safe, the two hustled to the hatchway and disappeared into the darkness below. In Conrad's hand were a lantern, a scissors, and jug of water, and Lena carried a towel, soap, and clothes for the orphans. Stealthily, the two crept toward the two barrels hiding the stowaways.

Conrad tapped softly on the wooden barrels as he called their names, and Jurgen and Kasimir emerged. Lena refrained from showing her astonishment at the appearance of the two boys as she hastily sat first Jurgen and then Kasimir on a box, putting them at her eye level. Carefully, she trimmed their ragged hair into cuts that looked somewhat professional. Conrad picked up clumps of dirty hair from the floor, leaving no evidence behind. Taking clothes from the Pollmanns' rucksacks, Lena had hoped to be able to wash the orphans' belongings and return the borrowed clothes to the children. Now, looking at the deplorable sight of the trousers and shirts, she had little hope of salvaging them. It would be a worry that she'd deal with later. With a rag and a jug of water and a piece of soap, Lena bathed the boys, wiping them with a small towel.

With all done in silence in less than an hour, the four were ready to emerge, and Conrad went first to survey the amidship area. A sailor was now keeping dogwatch, and Conrad hoped that the four could slip out when the sailor turned to survey the far amidship section.

Quietly relaying his plans to Lena, they were ready to emerge at the chosen moment. Conrad went first, pulling the boys up; however, the sailor turned earlier than expected, returning to the stern. Quickly, Conrad moved into the darkness with the boys, leaving Lena alone on the stairs in the bowels of the ship.

In the long minutes that followed, Conrad prayed that his sister-in-law was strong as she stood in the inky blackness of the rat-invested lower level. He glanced overhead, noticing that the post-midnight sky was fighting a patient battle with the dark clouds, which obstructed any stars that would add unwanted light. Within ten minutes, Conrad rushed to the hatchway to signal

Lena's escape. Trembling as she grabbed Conrad, her icy fingers wrapped around his hand as the four silently moved toward the steerage compartment.

* * * * *

On cat paws, the four entered the compartment, directing the boys to their two berths — number 99 and number 102 — now readied for the newcomers. Sharing with Christoph and Karl, the orphans quickly climbed to the top bunks. Lena hid their dirty clothes under her mattress, with plans to deal with them in the morning.

The orphans were silent as they closed their eyes and stretched their legs for the first time in two weeks. Although the berths were meager, they were far more than the boys had expected, and they nestled into the straw mattress with appreciation.

The day was still in the early stages of dawn when Conrad awoke, his thoughts reeling over the previous night. Unbeknownst to him, Lena had not slept at all, her mind filled with thoughts of the deplorable state of the two little boys. Her heart had instantly gone out to them, and as she crawled into her berth at 2 o'clock in the morning., she felt a stream of tears fall down her cheek.

Lena heard Elizabeth stir on the lower level of the compartment as she peeked into the upper berths. All the children were asleep except for Margaretha who blinked her eyes open briefly before rolling over. As Lena raised onto her elbow, she motioned Elizabeth toward her to whisper details about Jurgen and Kasimir. In a few minutes, Lena had pulled the tattered clothes from under her mattress, showing them to her sister. Quickly, Elizabeth scrutinized them, trying to fathom how she might mend them to make them wearable. Finally, she took the clothes from Lena, placing them under her pillow until she could wash them, unnoticed.

By 7 o'clock, all the adults had arisen and gathered their food rations for themselves and the children. With two extra mouths, the family would willingly divide their portions so that the shortage would hardly be noticeable. With blight in Germany the previous winter, many nights when at home in Hummersen, the Pollmanns had had less food than was supplied on the ship.

Barley bread, butter, and cheese were the norm for breakfast, and Kasimir and Jurgen's eyes were wide at the prospect of such a meal. With the shawl and Emma's small blanket covering a portion of the berths' openings, the boys crouched in the corner unnoticed by any passersby.

As the passengers were preparing to eat their meal, many of the people occupied the wooden benches that sat outside the compartment. The area was meant to give added sitting space for the steerage passengers, but at mealtime, it doubled as their "dining room." However, the Pollmanns often ate in their berths so they could talk privately. Thus, it wouldn't seem unusual if they stayed on their bunks this morning. Elizabeth — showing no sign of "morning sickness" today — cheerfully divided the food for the children.

In no time, the boys had won the hearts of the Pollmanns — Kasimir with his large, sad eyes and Jurgen with his strong, quiet resolve. Both had overcome so much in their short lives — hunger, fear, loneliness, and desertion by parents. And then life in the orphanage had been terrifying — beatings, neglect, and cruel labor.

When Kasimir had been beaten for dropping a crust of bread onto the filthy floor, the two decided to escape. The thought of being alone and running without food in the outside world could be no worse than the inner workings of the orphanage. Kasimir still had ugly wounds from the beating four weeks previously, and Elizabeth was the first to lovingly nurse them. A slash on his arm was red and infected — it was nasty when Elizabeth first applied ointment and bandages from the rucksack. Kasimir was, of course, unable to go to the compartment for sick patients — allegedly called a "hospital" — so Elizabeth did what she could with the supplies available.

* * * * *

With the sighting of four or five swordfish at dawn, it was rumored to be a sure sign of a restless sea, and sailors said that "all hell would break loose." Partially prepared for the worst, the passengers watched in the late afternoon as the sky became threatening with deep, dark clouds and fierce streaks of lightning. The *Don Quixote's* timbers moaned in undeniable agony. Because of the ship's rough movements, a barrel of water — not securely anchored to the floor — broke free, careening wildly across the compartment, shattering against a lower berth. With water spewing everywhere, the area was left soggy and wet.

To add to the chaos, as the Atlantic storm continued unabated, the hatchway to the stern was closed, permitting no one out and no fresh air in. As the steerage area grew more stale and polluted, people began to feel ill. No food or water was distributed, and steerage passengers went without supper as the afternoon slipped into evening and the storm continued. The Pollmanns had a few provisions in their rucksacks and, thus, fared better than most.

All night the storm raged, throwing the ship's belongings upside down. Passengers clutched to their berths in order not to be tossed into the throes of the ship. Finally, by morning, the gusty winds had slackened, the rain had ceased, and the sun seemed to be trying to peek from beneath the clouds. With the restless sea again calm, the passengers slowly came out of their berths for fresh air, food, and water. It was the dawn of March 24.

Before doing anything else, Elizabeth looked at Kasimir's wounds and found his arm still swollen and red. Applying fresh ointment and bandages, she felt his head and feared he was running a slight fever. Nevertheless, there was little else she could do except say a prayer and return from the washroom with a cold compress to lay on his forehead.

Slowly, the Pollmann children lowered themselves to the floor. It was still wet, and the wooden planks chilled their bare feet. The central aisle was cluttered with passengers' possessions that had been tossed to and fro during the storm. Many of the ladies were now stumbling through the aisle to get to the washroom, despising the privies even more this morning as they wondered about their condition after the storm.

Overall, the washroom area was worse than ever. With the hatchway closed all night, the stench was now unbearable. Passengers, who had gotten sick during the storm because of the thrashing of the sea, lay in their berths in a kind of stupor due to the air, which had been replaced by foul gases.

Most people who were not ill had already made their way to the stern or bow to fill their lungs with fresh sea air. As breakfast was passed out, those who felt like eating took their food and stood above deck, gazing at the now calm, turquoise sea and blue sky, which showed no indication of the dreadful storm only hours before.

Elizabeth and the girls returned from the washroom to their berths, finding plates of food — not only rye bread and butter but also dried apples — sitting on the bunks. Even milk was supplied that morning for the children — something they received only five days a week.

Even though the night had been frightening and interminably long, the sun was now starting to shine with the expected promise of a fresh, new day. It was this promise — this hope — of each new day that helped keep the morale of the passengers from falling too low when the conditions on the ship seemed less than satisfactory.

Nineteen

SICKNESS OF BOARD

Some days Kasimir seemed better than others, but Elizabeth was concerned that his wound was not healing properly.

"I understand why he wasn't healing quickly before he got to us, but he's getting better nutrition now. I don't understand why his arm is still red and swollen," Elizabeth said to Lena one day a week later.

"I'm baffled, too. I wish he could go above board and get fresh air," Lena replied. "Maybe we should try sneaking him out at night."

Elizabeth was hesitant. Fearing discovery of the stowaways, Elizabeth declined the suggestion, saying she felt they needed to remain in the berths. The two never complained and were simply grateful for food, water, a decent place to sleep, and, of course, companionship.

By the end of ten days, one-fourth of the passengers were ill and an alarming number had died — 20 out of 250 — most from the steerage compartments. Fever ran rampant. With no way to quarantine people, it was impossible to stop the spread of disease. Some passengers staggered up to the stern looking ghostly and hollow cheeked.

Passengers were most petrified about cholera. A severe bacterial infection of the gut caused by contaminated water, vomiting and diarrhea eventually caused dehydration and death. Entering various stages after the contraction of cholera, the victims went from intense thirst, extreme weakness, sunken eyes to decreased urination, weakened pulse, unconsciousness, seizures, and finally kidney failure. A torturous death, it was a misunderstood disease in the 1800s. Many believed that the disease was caused by "poisonous vapors." Believing it was the scourge of the depraved, poor masses, the steerage area of the ship seemed doomed.

"Local medicated bitters" were often administered, probably doing more harm than good. Simple fluids would have been the best treatment, but people of the 1800s didn't recognize that, and if the patients were given liquids, they were administered too little, too late, or too much, too quickly. However, survival rates were better than expected. It was puzzling why some people seemed very susceptible, some became sick but recovered, and others never succumbed at all to the dreaded disease. With no cases of cholera appearing in the Pollmanns' compartments, the adjoining compartment was contaminated, and, of course, the Pollmann family members were continually ill-at-ease.

Henrietta Wedermeyer, a young girl who had become Margaretha's friend, contracted cholera 16 days into the voyage. People began taking blankets and hanging them over the berth opening to provide privacy, making the Pollmanns' upper berths, which hid the orphans, less obvious. Not having seen Henrietta for several days, Margaretha saw her mother in the washroom one morning and inquired about her.

"Henrietta's ill, Margaretha. Very ill." With dark circles under her eyes, Margaretha could tell that Henrietta's mother had not slept in days. "Her fever is high, and I fear the worst," she sobbed. "I must return to her quickly."

Unable to say anything, Margaretha watched Mrs. Wedermeyer scurry from the washroom with wet cloths to be used as compresses on Henrietta.

With the hospital compartment already crammed, it was actually better for a patient to remain contained in her own berth. Almost anytime that a patient was sent to the "hospital," she worsened. Fever, cholera, and typhus all appeared in the hospital, and people began administering self-quarantine to the sick in their separate berths as much as possible.

* * * * *

One evening, the Pollmann children were playing a game — all crowded into Kasimir and Karl's upper berth. Kasimir seemed well enough that night to sit and play a game. Even though his arm still was not completely healed and his fever was still peaking at times, he was in good spirits this particular evening. The adults sat below on the benches and talked in jubilant tones as it had been a good day. No storms had arisen, Kasimir was better, and the food had been exceptional — bread, honey, potato soup, and sausage with kraut in the evening followed by dried figs for dessert. No one was ill in the Pollmann berths, and that was a special blessing to all.

Lena was the only one missing. She had made friends with several young people, and often in the evenings, she would spend time with them above deck. Isabella Schumacher, petite, blonde, and mischievous, was the same age as Lena — 19 — and her brother, Anton, was three years older. Already established in Hanover as a carpenter, Anton was leaving a good career to move to the New World. Tall and handsomely blonde, he knew he could re-establish himself in the carpentry profession wherever he settled. A cousin, Edith, who had worked in Hanover as a seamstress, had just turned 15 and was traveling with her two cousins to Indiana. There, they would meet with two uncles who had wives and children.

The Pollmanns were surprised to see Lena returning so early, and as she neared, they noticed she was crying.

"What is it Lena, darling?" Elizabeth asked.

Stifling her sobs so that the children couldn't hear, she relayed what she had witnessed.

"I had heard of burials at sea," she cried as she wiped her damp cheeks. "I just hadn't seen any. We were sitting on deck, and two sailors came forward with a board. At first I didn't know what they were carrying — it was a small package wrapped in white cloth. It was a body, of course, but I didn't know that."

Lena hesitated again as the ladies stared, awestruck. Elizabeth took Lena's hand in hers — it was cold and clammy — and she patted it gently.

"They lifted the board to the top rail, and with a grunt, the two sailors tilted the board up as the body slid off and plummeted into the sea." A stream of tears again rolled down Lena's face as she continued. "The family of the victim was wailing from behind, and I saw the wife of Heinz Stuckelmeyer. I believe it was their little daughter, Kathe, who had died. I heard last week that she was very ill."

Conrad and Christian had both seen this burial procedure on various occasions but had not relayed the experience to the ladies. Now, of course, their wives had heard first-hand from Lena, and it was not a pretty story.

"Ladies," Conrad inserted, "it's not a nice thought, but burial must be done this way. It's the kindest thing to do. They can't keep the bodies until we land. Think of the consequences."

Conrad's comment was followed by silence as each was wrapped in her own private thoughts. What if the Pollmanns would have to do such a burial? Elizabeth immediately tried to discard the impossible thought.

"None of us are ill, and..." Elizabeth hesitated, thinking of Kasimir, "and, well, God provides strength when we need it." Elizabeth looked up at Lena who had grown so fond of little Kasimir. "Lena, honey, sit with us."

"No, I think I'll go back to my friends." In a quick gesture, she hugged her sisters and disappeared to the stern.

An extra prayer was said that night for Kasimir who seemed to linger between ill health and grave sickness. It was now April 2 — nearly four weeks into their voyage — and never once had he been in a state of steady health since they found him.

Twenty

ILLNESS IN THE POLLMANN BERTH

Storms continued and so did burials. Conrad and Chris had heard the term "coffin ships" used even before they had left Hummersen. Believing it to be an exaggeration, they scoffed at the term. Now, however, the men saw at least one burial at sea per day, and they understood that disease running rampant with death close behind caused people to accurately name the vessels to America "coffin ships."

The previous night, Christian had seen the Wedermeyers weeping above board as two sailors dropped a small bundle into the sea. His heart tightened as he realized that Henrietta had succumbed to illness. Trying to block from his thoughts the fact that this could have been any one of the Pollmann children, he decided to refrain from mentioning the incident to anyone, especially the children.

April 5, almost four weeks at sea, dawned perfectly. A convalescent sun appeared — first weak but pale and by midday, bright — after a previously stormy day, and the sea glistened with sparkling ripples. The previously cold, gusty wind had warmed to a cool, brisk breeze, and life was better. They were perhaps a little more than four weeks from land.

The large burly doctor with broad shoulders and a generous mustache covering his fleshy cheeks was seen for the first time in weeks on deck. With his hands plunged deep into his pockets, he stood looking out at sea as if in thought about how many of his patients now resided there below. He deliberately avoided eye contact with passengers for fear of conversation.

On this morning, Lena walked casually with her three new-found friends, and Anton was at her side. She had formed a close relationship with the three, and they seemed a comfort to her after leaving her parents and close friends in Hummersen. Grateful for her sisters and their families, Lena still felt an emptiness, which was partially filled with Kasimir as well as with these young people from Hanover. Anton, in particular, seemed smitten by Lena and dropped by the compartment often at twilight to ask if she could stroll the deck. Isabella and Anton's parents had died the previous year with fever, and when the two decided to make a new life in America, they thought of going to the rolling, green hills of Wisconsin. Edith asked to join them. Her parents — frightened to let the 15-year-old child go — reluctantly cut the ties when Anton said they'd go instead to Indiana to be with other relatives. Farming in the northern part of Indiana, the relatives welcomed the prospect of German cousins joining them.

When Anton would come for Lena, Elizabeth noticed that her sister listened intently to his stories, her eyes glistening, and more than once, she anticipated that Lena was "falling in love."

"Time will tell, Elizabeth," Christian would say when his wife brought up the subject. "She's old enough to know her mind, and Anton seems like a gentleman."

Elizabeth nodded and smiled to Chris. "Of course, you're right, dear. I was younger than she when you came into my life and swept me off my feet." Elizabeth's impish grin made Christian blush, and he kissed her cheek.

"I think that it was the other way around. I had no intention of marrying for years, and I was overtaken by your charm and beauty," Christian concluded.

They laughed as he wrapped his arms around his wife in an embrace that happened all too seldom in those dismal days at sea. He could feel her slightly bulging belly, and placing his hand on it, they shared a smile.

* * * * *

By the next evening, Regina had suddenly become feverish, and Kasimir's temperature had risen alarmingly, putting him into a delirious state. His arm — still swollen — had red streaks striating up and down, originating from the still-open wound. There was no hiding either problem from the Pollmann children. With two sick, all hands were needed.

Elizabeth brought lemon balm, white willow, and lobelia from her rucksack to administer to both patients. Whenever Kisimir's fever peaked during the last weeks, Elizabeth or Lena had given him herbs in attempt to reduce his soaring temperature. Now, however, golden seal and yarrow poultice was put onto Kasimir's open wound, which was more alarming than his fever. The red streaks were a threatening sign but to call the doctor was risky.

"I think we need to chance it," Christian finally said. "I doubt that the doctor will ask questions. He'll assume that Kasimir's our son."

"Does he have to document those who are ill?" Elizabeth asked, trying to remain calm.

"Originally, the doctor wrote everything down, but I doubt it now. There's been so much sickness that I think the doctor only writes down deaths," Chris replied.

In the end — around 10 o'clock at night — Doctor Kolmeyer was summoned. Looking at Regina first, he administered a tablet of quinine and white willow and ordered cold compresses for her. Moving to the upper berth and examining Kasimir's wound, he shook his head. Immediately, Christian pulled him aside.

"What is it?" he asked.

"He needs amputation, and I don't have adequate operation facilities available tonight. Perhaps in the morning. Just keep him comfortable and apply poultices of olive oil and salts. Come by the hospital around 9 o'clock tomorrow morning."

Giving Christian some small containers with the "medicines," the doctor was gone, leaving Christian to absorb the shocking news and decide how much to tell the family.

Christian glanced at his wife who was a sickly pale, dodging first from Regina's side and then to Kasimir's berth. Returning for the um-teenth time to check on Regina, Elizabeth looked at her husband. By his expression, she knew that something was wrong.

"What is it, Chris?"

"The doctor left some medicine to apply as a poultice. We'll see how he is in the morning." Avoiding Elizabeth's eyes, Chris scurried into Kasimir's berth where he found Lena keeping constant vigil.

Christian was already convinced that no decision would have to be made at 9 o'clock the next morning. Lena had been joined by Margaretha, and it was difficult to keep the damp cloth cool as Kasimir's fever peaked to its limits. Chris handed them the latest poultice ingredients to be used on his swollen, ugly-looking wound. Young as Margaretha was, she had seen death with the farm animals, and a peculiar smell always permeated the air before the animal succumbed to its fate. That odor was present now as it filtered throughout the berth, and Christian was sure that both Margaretha and Lena were aware of it. He winced as he released the blanket to partially cover the opening and went again to look at Regina.

In contrast to Kasimir, Regina looked healthy although her usually bright green eyes seemed pale. She sipped rosemary tea with lemon as Louisa and Conrad talked quickly to her.

"How's Kasimir?" she asked as Christian peeked in. Her voice was raspy and weak, but it held a resolve that Christian had always noticed in the Haas sisters.

"Well, he has a fever, but he's tough." He tried to smile, but it was a feeble attempt. "We'll just wait and see how he is tomorrow."

Christian patted her hand, realizing that possibly the fever had broken because it had cooled. "Call me in a couple of hours, and I'll relieve you," he said to Conrad and Louisa. They nodded.

"Good night, Regina," Chris said as he turned to find Elizabeth.

They talked quietly before retiring, both deciding to get up in a few hours to relieve the four who stood watch. However, shortly after midnight when Elizabeth went to relieve Lena, she refused to go.

"No, I want to stay. Margaretha, you go to bed, and your mother and I will stay watch."

"Lena, you have been at Kasimir's bedside all day and night. You need some rest," Elizabeth argued.

"No, Elizabeth. I'm going to stay. It won't be much longer." A solitary tear rolled down her face as she took his small, fragile, burning hand to her lips.

Twenty-one

BURIAL AND FIRE AT SEA

April 6 dawned with damp expectancy. It was a dull, gray day and seemed to be dying even as it was born. The Pollmanns husbanded their strength as they looked at Kasimir in the still darkened steerage. The red streaks now covered his arm and his breathing was shallow and labored. The children were kept from his berth as Elizabeth and Lena sat with him through his twilight hours. At around 8 o'clock, Elizabeth emerged whispering that it was over and that Louisa should get soap and water so that he could be bathed.

Lena's courage and bravery resounded as she washed little Kasimir. His tiny, frail face had an expression of peace that she had never seen, and despite the stabbing pain that she felt in her heart, she was glad that his struggle was over. What a wretched life he had led — all five years of it — and now for the first time, he lay bathed in tranquil bliss.

Dreading the concept of telling Jurgen, Christian hesitated going to his berth. But nothing had to be said, as Jurgen knew as soon as he saw Christian's face.

"Kasimir is dead." It was a statement from Jurgen rather than a question, and Christian nodded. "I'm glad because he was so very sick. He knew that he wasn't going to live," Jurgen said, his eyes downcast.

"What do you mean?" Chris questioned.

"He had a dream a week ago. He was watching as someone carried a white bundle onto the open deck. He saw Lena crying and someone asked her what was wrong. She said, 'Kasimir died.'"

Christian stood silently, wondering how the children knew about the "white bundle." No one had mentioned it to them as the means of burying the dead. Somehow, though, Kasimir had known and had shared it with Jurgen.

Conrad — his face a study of agony — went in search of material to wrap little Kasimir for burial. He didn't dare ask for burial cloth as a death would have to be reported and so they decided to hold a private ceremony after midnight. It was all of their fervent hope that the stars would be absent and the waves would be slashing against the boat, so that it would help disguise the funeral.

Near the hospital compartment, Conrad found cloth — plentiful and unguarded. One piece was ample for the small, frail body, and he tucked it inside his waistcoat. When he returned, Conrad found his wife sitting up with Louisa at her side. For the moment, Regina was better, and Louisa was attempting to feed her some bread soaked in milk. She tried to smile, and Conrad wondered if she had been given the news of Kasimir.

Elizabeth, feeling weak and nauseated after the long vigil, had taken to bed. Lena sat near Kasimir, bathing him, stroking his head, and praying over his body. Unable to bare the thought of wrapping him in the white cloth, she folded it at the foot of the berth to await the evening hours.

The day passed with heavy-lidded eyes as if it — along with the Pollmanns — mourned Kasimir's death. No rain fell, but the sun was obscured by dark clouds, and the view across the sea was heavy with haze. The Pollmanns remained in their berths, talking quietly or resting. By 9 o'clock, the moon — four days shy of being full — poked through the cloud cover for a short time before it retreated for the remainder of the night. Stars were blanketed from view, and so the midnight sky was an inky black when Christian and Conrad made their way to the rail with the small bundle.

An hour earlier, the Pollmanns had gathered to conduct a quiet "funeral," with Christian leading the prayers in the upper berth. In the early evening, Lena and Elizabeth had wrapped the body, and Lena was determined to stay strong and courageous even though she felt as if her heart had been ripped apart.

"The Lord always has reasons, and His decisions are never wrong," Elizabeth had reminded her sister. Lena nodded as Elizabeth pulled the cloth tighter around the cold, limp body, and Lena held the short strips of rope to tie the small white bundle.

* * * * *

April 7 dawned a new day. The coquettish weather had become sunny again, and the cold air seemed to have spent itself, replaced by a slightly warm breeze. Regina had endured a restless night with a rising and falling fever, but she arose again for breakfast. Resolute that life would go on, the Pollmann family said their prayers before starting the new day, and Conrad and Christian went above deck to breathe fresh air.

Consulting a first-mate about the possible duration of the voyage, they were told that they wouldn't see land for another four or five weeks. Jubilant that the voyage was almost half over, they stood for perhaps half an hour chatting with fellow passengers and were about to retreat to their compartment when a small man approached them. Middle-aged with sly eyes and a drooping black mustache, he looked directly at Christian.

"Kasimir died, didn't he?"

Astounded, Christian exchanged glances with Conrad. He searched for an answer, but it wouldn't come.

Finally, Conrad responded. "Sir, what do you mean?" It was the best Conrad could do as he stalled for time.

"Kasimir, the orphan, he died" was the reply. It was not a question but a statement.

"Who are you?" Christian had finally found his tongue and asked the inevitable question that both he and Conrad were wondering.

"I'm a friend — Guido."

Guido…Guido. The man who originally helped Jurgen and Kasimir. They had tried to locate him from the orphans' description, but it had been futile.

Unable to ask too many questions for fear of unearthing knowledge about the stowaways, Chris and Conrad eventually gave up finding the lost friend.

Now, here he was. Small and frail himself, his sly eyes turned soft as he stared in solemn repose at the two men.

"Yes, he died. We buried him at sea at midnight," Christian answered. "How did you know?"

"I've kept track of the boys after you helped them. I knew where they were but didn't want to visit for fear of making a commotion. Now, I wish I had," Guido responded in remorse.

"Would you like to see Jurgen?" Conrad asked.

"Not now; maybe later. I'll come to your berths."

As fast as he appeared, Guido was gone. He slipped around the hatchway and disappeared.

Christian and Conrad stood staring, both thinking the same thought — if Guido knew where the boys were and that Kasimir had died, how many others knew of the secret? Did Guido only know because he had been watching or was the stowaways' presence well known? Should they tell the ladies about the encounter with Guido?

While sitting and discussing the questions, the two decided it best not to immediately disclose the morning's news of Guido. Too much had happened, and Regina was still ill.

"Later will be better," Conrad said as the two arose to descend into the hatchway.

* * * * *

Days progressed well for Regina, and by April 9, she was up and fulfilling her normal duties with the children. Elizabeth, occasionally experiencing a bit of morning sickness, never slacked from helping. With much spare time on the ship, the ladies took turns with lessons to keep the children occupied. The Pollmann and Haas families alike had always been in favor of education — all stressing it with their children. Now as they crossed the Atlantic, the family felt sure that schooling would most certainly be an essential part of their children's lives in America.

It was midday of the 9th when an alarm of "fire" went up. It was from the amidship section where a group of card-playing men — all smoking — had been sitting on bails of straw. A lighted match had been dropped into a nearby bail, and fire had begun undetected. Passersby saw the flames and shouted the alarm. A fresh wind fanned the flames, which spread quickly to another bail.

Hearing the chaos above, the steerage passengers stood in shock, thinking of the dreadful sight of the *Columbus* bound for New York, which they had seen weeks before. With 400 passengers aboard, misfortune fell early on the *Columbus'* voyage. Only two weeks at sea, fire in the forward hold was reported. While the crew battled the flames, some of the frantic passengers took matters into their own hands and lowered life boats into the turbulent sea. In a chaotic scene, they lowered themselves into the water, and ten people drowned before the rest clamored back to safety.

The fire on the *Columbus* raged all night until water-logged holds prevented it from spreading, but the crew knew the vessel was doomed. A red flag signifying distress had been hoisted soon after the fire started, and everyone prayed that a ship would pass by to rescue them. A day before the *Don Quixote* had reached the *Columbus*, look-out men on the *Conquerer* — a ship sailing from Canada to London — had spotted the *Columbus*. Within two hours the *Conquerer* had pulled up to the *Columbus* as a darkened sky triggered a full-fledged gale, which lasted the rest of the day and into the night. Because of the horrific winds and rain, the *Conquerer* was unable to rescue the passengers of the doomed ship, and many died before the storm abated. When the *Don Quixote* finally arrived, the passengers who had survived the storm had been dragged aboard the *Conquerer* and the *Columbus* now was a sinking, burning wreckage.

Although the mishap had occurred weeks before, the sight of the *Columbus* was still fresh in the minds of the passengers of the *Don Quixote*, and Christian knew it was paramount that people didn't panic. He tried to talk to people in the steerage as Conrad climbed the hatchway to attain information. In ten minutes, he returned to say that the fire was under control by the crew but not without some damage to the amidship area.

When night fell and a weak moon showed in the sky, Christian went to survey the deck, finding a large section had been roped off and repair had already begun. Other men stood silently on deck, also examining the damage done by the fire.

Christian remained for perhaps half an hour and was about to leave when he focused on a conversation of two men next to him. He had paid no attention until the stocky man dressed in a clean, fashionable suit said in an exasperated voice, "I can't believe he's dead. Did someone find him just this morning?"

Obviously from the first-class section, the stocky man rubbed his balding head and was seemingly quite upset. Christian's first thought was that disease had spread to the upper class. Nonetheless, he stood listening.

"Yes, his brother found him before breakfast," the other gentleman answered, his face taut and his black eyes piercing. "Ignatius usually got up by 7 o'clock to eat, and when he wasn't up at 8 o'clock, Fritz, knocked on the door. When Ignatius didn't answer, he opened it slightly. He was horrified to find Ignatius' pajama top literally soaked in blood. His throat had been slit."

Shocked, Christian attempted to hide his surprise and not let the gentlemen know he had heard the conversation.

"Now, not a word, Johannes, because the officials are trying to keep it a secret. They're searching for clues of the murderer so…."

Out of earshot, the two men walked toward first-class, the stocky man using a cane in his left hand to steady himself. They stopped again for a few seconds, absorbed in conversation, then continued on. Christian stared after them, wondering what it all meant and trying to decide what to do with his new-found knowledge. A murderer on board? And he could be any one of the passengers. Did he murder for money or did he kill for no reason, making any person on board ship his next victim? Christian finally walked slowly toward the hatchway. It was April 9, Maundy Thursday. It was the start of the most holy, solemn week in all Christians' calendar and most definitely an important religious time for the Pollmanns. Should he relay the murder to Conrad or keep it secret until after Easter? Christian pondered the question as he descended into the steerage area.

Twenty-two

JURGEN POLLMANN

Without deliberation, Christian decided to keep the information silent until after Easter. Although he was worried that a murderer could be in their very midst, Christian didn't want to ruin an Easter weekend.

Because of the illnesses and death, Lena had seen very little of her friends, but Easter weekend was a time of worship, and on Good Friday, Anton asked if he could join the family. Perched on the top berths, the family sang hymns and prayed as the sun arose overhead, marking the 12 o'clock hour of Christ's death. Jurgen, who had received strict religious lessons at the orphanage, was proud to lead a final prayer for Kasimir. He had made a crude wooden cross from sticks for Kasimir, and a single tear dropped on his straw mattress as Jurgen attached the cross to the berth with a piece of string. The simple gesture tugged at Elizabeth's heart as she sat watching.

Weeks before Kasimir had become ill, she and Christian had discussed what would become of the two orphans once they arrived in America. They had decided to take Jurgen as their own with the prospect of Lena taking her beloved Kasimir. Even though Elizabeth was now certainly pregnant, they both loved the adorable orphan, who showed a sound resolve to conquer any obstacle in life.

At first sad and solemn, Jurgen proved to have a quick smile and fast wit given the opportunity. Having been dropped off at the orphanage at age four, his parents had died in a fire. Elizabeth expected he had had a good life up until then, and his bright, sunny personality re-emerged as his days were filled with genuine love. Anna-Marie — her eyes sparkling when her father lifted her to the top berth — already clung to Jurgen as if he were an older brother.

*   *   *   *   *

Easter Sunday — April 12 — dawned a picture postcard day. The round, yellow sun glistened on the aquamarine Atlantic, and the passengers were jubilant on this most holy Sunday. A special breakfast of rye bread, oat biscuits with honey, and dried peaches with cream were served. Second helpings were allowed as various passengers took turns in leading favorite hymns. For once, Protestants and Catholics worshipped together with no rivalry. Many parents had attempted to make small Easter presents for their children using such things as cloth, candies, dried flowers, and ribbons found in their rucksacks. It was a glorious day, and one that was needed after four weeks of trials at sea.

The Pollmann family celebrated that afternoon with baby Maria as she sat alone for the first time. She had turned seven months and was inquisitive, healthy, and happy despite the conditions of the ship. Regina — back to her normal self after the bout with the fever — held the baby much of the time, shielding her from the rough straw mattress.

Since Kasimir's death, Lena tried to spend more time with her nieces and nephews. Death has a way of jolting everyone into seeing how brief life can be, and Lena wanted the children to realize how important they were to her. Not talking about Kasimir, Lena was still in deep grief, but she always attempted to harbor her sadness from her family. However, sometimes at night, Elizabeth heard a soft whimper and knew that her sister was crying.

It was one night soon after Elizabeth first heard the muffled sobs of Lena that she laid awake in one of her sleepless nights. Often contemplating what life would be like in the New World, Elizabeth rolled and tossed on her straw mattress. In the stillness of that night, Elizabeth heard an infant's crying coming from the adjoining compartment.

Reaching down to Christian's berth, she woke him. "Chris, there's a baby crying. Do you think that Marta has had her baby?"

Marta Baumgartner was a young mother from the inner city of Berlin. Trying to escape the hunger and filth of the big, overcrowded city, she and her family were going to join an uncle living in Pennsylvania. Expecting her third child, Marta wasn't due to deliver for another four weeks. Hoping to be in New York when she gave birth, Marta had endured the voyage well with only minor complications.

Arising, Christian — already in trousers — pulled on his shirt and walked the 15 feet to the next compartment. The doctor's large body was apparent as he sat on Marta's berth. Wanting Marta to stay out of the still-infected hospital compartment, the doctor had delivered the baby in berth #89. Marta's sister, Helga, was washing the squalling little boy as Marta's husband, Otto, beamed at his third son.

Well into the night, the baby continued to cry, and Elizabeth finally arose at 4 o'clock to see if Marta needed help. Frantic that she had no milk yet, Marta had sent her sister in search of Heidi, a mother with a two-month-old infant. Having already nursed her baby, Heidi came as quickly as possible to help Marta with her newborn. It was to no avail as he screamed relentlessly into the morning hours. The baby wouldn't nurse from Heidi, and nothing seemed to soothe the child.

Exhausted, Marta fell into a light sleep, and when she awoke, there was silence. Marta called her sister, who slowly appeared cradling a small bundle in her arms. With no possible explanation, the newborn had suddenly stopped breathing and succumbed to death within a matter of minutes.

Marta was inconsolable — drowned in grief. Otto tried to comfort her, but it was fruitless, and days after the baby had received his sea burial, Marta sobbed uncontrollably. Her two other young sons attempted to talk with her, but her depression deepened, and two weeks later — overcome with grief — Marta breathed her last. Stunned and overwhelmed with shock, Otto and the boys now faced their new life in America alone.

On the morning of April 20 — when the sun was hesitant and the breeze was cool — Marta Baumgartner received a sea burial. With approximately three weeks of the voyage left, the steerage passengers looked out over the Atlantic Ocean, which had now claimed 60 of the 250 travelers.

* * * * *

Christian continued to ponder over the death of the man named Ignatius, and for the first week after he had heard of the murder, he had remained silent, not telling even Conrad the information. Going above board as often as possible, he stood near men engaged in conversation, hoping to learn more. Apparently, it was a well-kept secret because he heard nothing.

Christian had almost decided it had been a rumor. Ready to descend the hatchway for lunch one midday, Christian heard a regal-looking gentleman with white hair and a well-trimmed mustache saying, "Fritz said Ignatius died after experiencing chest pains, but I don't believe it. No doctor was there that day."

Christian stopped dead and pretended to drop something as he eased away from the hatchway. With his back to the two men, he was still within earshot as he stood looking out at the open sea, straining to hear the conversation.

"I heard commotion going on in Ignatius' compartment late in the morning, but no one was allowed near," responded the other gentleman. Younger and also distinguished looking, he had rimmed glasses sitting on his nose as he puffed on his pipe. "Truly, I don't know if a doctor was there or not, and I have no idea what happened to Ignatius. I barely knew the man. I was told that he was buried at sea the next night."

"He was murdered." The voice came from behind Christian.

Turning, Christian saw a third man join the conversation. Not having the appearance of a first-class passenger, Chris wondered who he was. Dressed in a faded black shirt, he had a hat pulled low over his eyes. A shaggy black beard was the most prominent feature on his face. Christian stared at him, but decided he had never seen him in the steerage class. Who was he?

"I beg your pardon," the older white-haired gentleman said.

"He was murdered. I overheard Fritz talking yesterday to the first-mate. They're looking for the murderer," the black-bearded man replied.

The three men seemed to know each other as they became engaged in a private conversation as they lowered their voices. Not able to understand the muffled words and not wanting to look obvious, Christian felt he couldn't move closer without being noticed. Soon the three moved away into the crowd, slipping out of Christian's sight and earshot.

All day, Christian's mind drifted back to the conversation, and he finally decided to relay the event to Conrad.

"A murder!" Conrad exclaimed after Christian had pulled him aside while they stood on the bow of the ship that evening.

Chris nodded.

"Are you sure?"

Christian told the story as he knew it. A bit astounded, Conrad was silent for a while, thinking.

"You know, something is starting to make sense. I heard a conversation a few days ago," Conrad responded.

With raised eyebrows, Christian listened.

"I heard a strange fellow talking. He said that the compartment was a mess when Fritz found his brother. Blood was everywhere. That's all I heard," Conrad concluded. " I had no idea what he meant and sort of forgot about it until now."

"What did the man look like?" Christian asked.

"He had piercing eyes, dark hair, and an untrimmed black beard."

Christian had been unable to see the man's eyes well because of the hat, but the black beard fit.

"Had you seen him before?" Chris asked.

"I think I saw him once before above board, but I'm not sure," Conrad responded.

The conversation was cut short as Anton and Lena approached, but later the two decided to watch for the bearded stranger as well as keep a tight vigil on their families.

＊ ＊ ＊ ＊ ＊

It was the evening of April 29, a little more than two weeks after Easter. Almost balmy all day, the sun was orange on the horizon, and a fair easterly wind blew across the Atlantic. The children were singing when the captain of the ship appeared at the door of the compartment. Christian had spoken on several occasions to the man, and he had seemed polite but not especially personable. Tonight his lips were turned into a snarl, and his dark looks were formidable.

The family had gotten lax about keeping Jurgen hidden. After Kasimir had died, it was difficult to contain him constantly, and Christian often took him above board in the evenings after the sun had set.

"You're hiding a stowaway." The captain's voice was gruff, and his eyes shot daggers through the dim light as he focused on Christian.

No one moved; no one spoke.

"Which boy is he?" The captain's hand shot out and grabbed four-year-old Karl by the scruff of his neck.

Louisa covered her mouth as she emitted a gasp, as Christian spoke in a strong, commanding voice.

"Sir, that's Karl, my nephew. Don't hurt him, please." As the captain lowered his hand, Christian continued. "You're right, sir. We did have a stowaway, but he's not on the run anymore. He belongs to my wife and me, and I'll gladly pay for his passage."

Taken aback by the response, the captain stared at Christian for a moment, his face softening a bit.

Christian quickly plunged his hand into his pocket, knowing that he didn't have 50 extra Talers for Jurgen's ticket. He had money for travel from New York City to the Midwest and to get started on a farm, but he didn't have an additional 50. However, he would worry about that later. The important thing was to keep little Jurgen who all had learned to love as their own.

By now, Jurgen had peeked his head out to look at the man with the intimidating voice. Jurgen's black curls fell over his eyes, which were now filled with fear.

"I'm here," his meek voice sounded from the upper berth. "Don't punish them because of me."

Conrad had already found 15 Talers, and Louisa and Lena each gave 5. With Christian's 25, they had a total of 50, and the coins lay in Chris' hand as he extended them to the captain.

"Don't take Jurgen from us, Captain," Elizabeth pleaded as she stepped forward aggressively. "He has had a difficult life in an orphanage, and my husband and I will care for him in America. He's our son now."

Quickly, Christian opened the large hand of the captain and placed 50 gold Talers into his palm.

Silence ensued, and then without so much as an answer, the captain turned on his heel and stalked out, the coins clutched in his massive hand. Unable to speak, the family seemed in shock for several seconds. Elizabeth was the first to respond as she looked at Jurgen.

"Well, son, you're ours now. Jurgen Pollmann — sounds pretty good, huh?"

Jurgen reached his tiny hand out to her. "Thank you. Oh, thank you so much."

Tears streamed down his face as Margaretha pulled him to her in a bear hug.

"I always wanted a brother, Jurgen," she shouted with excitement.

"And already big," chimed in tiny Anna-Marie, giggling with glee.

Twenty-three

PREPARE FOR LANDING

May 1 was anything but a beautiful spring May Day. A turbulent storm arose as the fog and mist turned into icy cold rain, and violent waves whipped the ship fiercely. With every wave the ship rose only to drop into a new pit of dark seawater with sprays of ice water fired in all directions. Shrieks of fear from the passengers were followed by moans as the rolling sea caused new bouts of seasickness. As the seawater lashed against the deck, the passengers buried themselves deeper into their berths, clinging to the bunk posts for stability.

For two hours the storm raged, and finally as it calmed, those who weren't ill went to the amidship, recently repaired after the fire. The men stood on the deck viewing the fickle, unpredictable ocean. Christian went alone above board as the rest of the family remained in the steerage, unwilling to face the volatile winds, which seemed to be in a continual erratic state. As he stood looking out at the capricious Atlantic Ocean, Christian's glance focused on the flags as they fluttered in the wind, still blowing from the recent assault.

Even as a child, Christian had always had a fascination with flags. When he and his father went into Schwalenberg, to the farmers' market, Christian liked to stand and watch the colorful flags flying from the Town Hall. There was something about the flapping sound that intrigued Christian, and when he boarded the *Don Quixote*, he had learned from the first-mate that identification flags were flown on each ship. The government registration issued ten colored flags representing numbers from zero to nine, and each ship flew four flags corresponding to her registration number. The number one was signified by a white flag with a blue square, five by a red flag, and eight by a blue flag with a yellow square. *Don Quixote's* identification number was 8515; thus, a series of four flags corresponding to that number were flown at the bow. Below the flags stood the figurehead — the golden female ornament, which helped guard the ship from the ocean's dangers. Little Anna-Marie loved the vibrant colors of the flags and the bright, golden figurehead, so Chris would often carry her onto the deck and hold her as she laughed and clapped at the flapping colors in the wind. It brought back good memories of his childhood days watching the Schwalenberg flags.

As Christian stood gazing at the flags that he could so often hear in the steerage during a storm, his glance fell upon the black-bearded man with piercing eyes who was standing beneath the flags. It was the first time in days that he'd seen the man who had previously declared Ignatius had been murdered. Still dressed in a rather ragged fashion, he was walking quickly toward the stern. In a determined attempt to follow him, Christian stumbled over a rucksack lying on deck. When he regained his footing, the stranger had disappeared, seemingly swallowed by the mingling crowd. He searched the deck for perhaps ten minutes, but the stranger had completely vanished, leaving Christian standing on the amidship section, perplexed. It had been a chance to follow the stranger, and he had bungled it.

* * * * *

Now as they entered their seventh week on board, word buzzed that land was near — only a few days away. The crowd was growing anxious — every passenger was restless to disembark from the ship that had held him prisoner for nearly two months. Christian was no different; however, he knew that this had been a part of life that he'd never forget. It was May 4, and like magic, the weather seemed to have changed. The storms had ceased, and an almost balmy breeze blew.

Christian imagined that the yellow crocus would now be a solid carpet on the hillside of Hummersen, and tulips would be sprouting their red, yellow, and white buds. For a moment he felt a pang of homesickness as he thought of his father and siblings left behind in Germany. A new life awaited him and his family, though, and soon he'd see his brother, Fredrich. He thought of the excitement that Louisa and her children must be anticipating after not having seen Fredrich in nearly two years.

And then Christian thought of Lena and the news that she had announced the previous evening — Anton had proposed. Giddy with excitement, she had answered "yes." Even though her sisters had anticipated this event, they still felt the thrill of the moment and sat talking long into the night. The Haas and Pollmann families were growing and changing — they had been lucky that they had come through the treacherous voyage unscathed and would enter the "New World" together as an entire unit with even more members added — Jurgen and now Anton and his family.

Now as morning chores were finished, the ladies along with the children joined Christian at the bow. Immediately, the women noticed that something was different. The air seemed to have a new odor — sweet — like the smell of green grass, trees, and earth. Other passengers noticed it as well and began to chatter incessantly. Were they truly close to land? Were they really about to embark upon America?

Within the hour, the captain — now in good trim and revealing a white toothy smile — announced that they would commence cleaning the steerage area in preparation for landing. Unable to believe that the long-awaited time had come, a cheer went up as the passengers stood on the bow, searching for the first sight of green land. Waves sprayed the travelers, but they didn't care — their journey was nearly completed. The captain was taking his place on the ratline to be seen, and the passengers quickly honored him by silence.

"Listen carefully all of you. Today will be spent scouring and swathing the steerage area. The American inspectors must see a sparkling clean ship when we arrive. Soap, water, and vinegar will be given to all of you in the steerage, along with buckets, brushes, and mops. First, you'll scrub and then mop. First-mates Shermer and Hoffmann will judge if your work is satisfactorily done. After the area has been scoured, you will throw all dirty clothes overboard. Nothing unclean must remain on the ship. Mattresses, clothing, shoes — anything soiled."

There was rumbling among the crowd that some people would be throwing everything they owned overboard.

"We have no clean clothes, sir," one steerage passenger finally had the courage to shout.

"Everything soiled must go," the captain snapped. "If the inspectors don't approve of you, you'll be sent back to Germany. It's your choice." The captain's smile had faded, and his cold eyes and snarl had returned.

Most people had brought new clothes in their rucksacks especially for this occasion; however, many had had to use all of their clothing because of unforeseen accidents, and now they were left with nothing. Some would be willing to pay other passengers for anything new and so soon swapping and trading would commence in the steerage compartments.

"One more thing before you leave," the captain yelled with cold, penetrating eyes. "There was been no sickness aboard the *Don Quixote*. No one has been hospitalized or died. The doctor will answer the questions asked by the inspector, but if you should be asked, you now know your answer." He paused. "The consequences will be that you'll all be returned to Germany if you refuse to answer as told." He looked closely at the crowd. "Are there any questions?" His gruff voice could be readily heard over the slapping of the waves as they hit the bow.

Ignoring the last comment, a passenger asked, "When exactly will we land?"

"We'll see land soon." It was an ambiguous answer.

Questions were whispered throughout the passengers. How soon? Tomorrow? Next week? Tonight? The immigrants wanted it clarified, but the captain jumped down from the ratline and was gone.

An excited crowd discussed what they had heard. Nothing was as important as the words "We'll see land soon."

And then another shout went up. "Seaweed," the young man cried.

He was holding a stringy green strand in his hand — it was something that he had grabbed after a wave had hit the deck. "It's green seaweed. Land is near!"

Peels of laughter and merriment shook the upper deck until they heard the intimidating, gruff voice from below. "Get to work — I mean now and not later, you good-for-nothing ruffians."

Clamoring to get below, the passengers for the first time in weeks felt rested, well, and full of life — the sweet scent of America was at hand.

Twenty-four

NEW YORK CITY HARBOR

By evening, the steerage compartment area was scoured to a sparkling clean. The *Don Quixote* not only looked incredibly clean but it also smelled fresh. The stale, musty air that had inhabited the steerage section for so many weeks had disappeared, replaced by the smell of soap and water. The filth that had seemed to be permanently ground into the floor was gone. The first-mates had approved, and the passengers were rewarded with additional helpings of bread, rice, and pork. It was a grand celebration as the passengers stood late into the night searching the black horizon for their future.

When the sun arose, they hoped they could at last bid farewell to the dark, loathsome sea that had thrashed them to and fro for two months and would at last see the green, solid earth of America. It was a restless night — one in which some never went to bed. Singing could be heard on the amidship all night as many of the travelers wanted to see the heavenly earth when the first rays of golden sun lit the sky.

Just before the sun peaked, the horizon was sparkling with faded but real gaslights — New York City was before them. It was May 5.

* * * * *

Within the next fifteen minutes, word spread quickly to the steerage that New York City was within sight, and soon the upper deck was crammed with passengers, all straining to view the amazing sight. The "New World" was whispered over and over in hushed tones.

Most passengers who had not already changed clothes now rushed below to strip off their soiled, ragged attire and donned whatever they could find that was more suitable. In an unceremonious gesture, the tattered shirts, trousers, and dresses were all tossed into the whirlpool below, which carelessly swallowed them in one gulp.

By afternoon on May 5, the *Don Quixote* eased its way through the harbor waters of New York City and dropped anchor at Staten Island. Excitement ran high, yet the 175 passengers that survived the Atlantic voyage were quiet on deck as they surveyed the scene. Silently, many of them offered thanks to God for their arrival, and others asked for strength and guidance after leaving one or more of their family to the cruel Atlantic. Having been accustomed to hearing the sounds of the ship — the timbers that continually creaked, the waves that washed against the sides, and the winds that moaned day and night — the passengers now listened to the eerie silence.

It was late evening when the sky started to darken and the gaslights of New York City could again be seen from the ship. It was then that Mr. Wolfe, the American inspector, came aboard to look at the *Don Quoxite*.

"Welcome aboard, Mr. Wolfe," Christian heard the captain say in a most pleasant tone of voice, seldom heard in the past two months. Gone were the snarling lips, replaced by his toothy smile.

"Captain Schwartz," Wolfe answered, nodding a greeting. "Nice to see you. Pleasant voyage?"

"Of course," the captain answered, throwing a sideways glance at the passengers to his left, making sure they were listening.

"Any illness or deaths?" Mr. Wolfe asked.

"Doctor Kolmeyer will answer that question." The captain nodded in the direction of the doctor, who was dressed in a sparkling white surgical coat, never seen before by the passengers. His shoulders thrown back and a professional stance taken, the doctor held his medical ledger in front of him.

"Typical complaints, but nothing unusual, sir," Doctor Kolmeyer answered in a matter-of-fact way, pretending to page through his ledger.

"Wonderful," Mr. Wolfe continued. "Any stowaways to your knowledge?"

"I thought I had one," the captain replied, "but it turned out to be an error."

"How so?" questioned Mr. Wolfe as he took notes in a small black pad.

The captain hesitated for a moment. "He was an adopted child that I hadn't seen previously," he stammered. "He was paid for so it was my mistake. Don't make many errors, you know," the captain replied, covering his nervousness with a smile.

The three entertained a laugh as Christian watched the captain tapping his foot with agitation. Apparently, however, Mr. Wolfe paid no attention as the conversation continued unabated.

"We'll just check below," Mr. Wolfe said as several other suit-clad men had now joined him on deck for the inspection.

Anxious about what the inspectors would find below in the steerage, the passengers talked quietly among themselves. Unbeknownst to the travelers, the inspectors were invited to dine with the captain and crew — a late-night bite of delicacies and ale saved especially for this occasion. As several hours elapsed, the passengers became restless — panicky, actually — as to what was happening below, and several men volunteered to sneak down in an attempt to see what was happening. With no one in sight, the men crept about the steerage area until they heard laughter in the captain's dining room and realized that dinner was being served. Ascending to the main deck, the news quickly spread, and although the steerage-class people were relieved, they felt deceived by the captain, who must have known their anxiety yet casually and leisurely entertained the inspectors

"He could have told us," Christian heard a passenger remark.

"Indeed," answered another. "He's snobbish and self-centered, always looking down on us. We're Germans just like him, you know."

It was near midnight when the captain and inspectors finally appeared, each holding a lantern to light the way. The sky had clouded, obscuring the moon and stars, and lightning was leaving threads of long, jagged white light in the western sky. Already the wind was howling fearfully and drops of rain were falling on the tired, weary passengers. As the inspectors descended into the awaiting boat below, the captain made an announcement to the people.

"We're going to wait until daybreak to go ashore. A storm is brewing, and we can't dock tonight."

Moans were heard, and as a scowl formed on the captain's partially lighted face, the sounds dissolved.

"It's your last night aboard so sleep well. You'll all need rest for tomorrow. New York City is rough, and only the strongest will survive," the captain retorted.

It was a typical statement for the cynical captain to make but an unnecessary one. Already frightened to enter a foreign country, the German passengers would have appreciated some encouraging words, but the captain had never made an effort to make the voyage any easier than necessary so they would have expected no less from him now.

In reality, most were glad to be protected from the storm and not thrown into New York City at midnight with inclement weather. Many mattresses had been thrown overboard so those people slept on the cold, wooden bunks. "It's only for one more night" was heard throughout the steerage as mothers encouraged their children to get ready for bed. "Tomorrow we'll set foot in the New World."

Few slept well again that night, and by 6 o'clock, the gray light of morning began to swell in the steerage compartment. It was May 6, 1852 — the day of disembarking. It was time to say goodbye to German friends met on the *Don Quixote*, and at last face the occasion they had all anticipated — stepping onto American soil and viewing their future.

Twenty-five

LIFE IN NEW YORK CITY'S "KLEINDEUTSCHLAND"

Suddenly, the Don Quixote was being towed by steamers to the inner harbor of New York City. The sea gulls dipped down to whisk pieces of bread from the passengers before sailing back up into the cloudless blue sky. It was a time of merriment.

As the gangplank was released, a band of twelve seedy fellows — sharks — scrambled aboard, all proclaiming to have rooms, work, and food for anyone who was willing to go with them. The Pollmanns kept tight grips on their children as the family descended the gangplank, all the while ignoring the sharks. Clutched in his hand, Conrad had not only the address of a clean, reasonably priced hotel, but also the place to retrieve their trunks, which had been sent several weeks prior to their departure.

Despite all of the worrying about the trunks arriving in New York City when they were going to arrive in New Orleans, the change in ship plans worked for the best. At least they hoped so. If the trunks hadn't been shipped off yet for the Midwest, the men could simply retrieve them, putting them onto the boat that they'd take to Chicago.

Anton, Isabella, and Edith clung close to the Pollmanns. Heading for Indiana, Anton knew whatever boat the Pollamnns took would be sufficient for them as well. Naturally, Lena had decided to continue to Indiana instead of Illinois. Not wanting to part from her sisters, she knew that she must because her place was now with Anton.

Little Jurgen was frightened as were the other children, but he was also excited — ecstatic is a better word — to enter the future with his new family. Holding tightly to Elizabeth's and Margaretha's hands, he strutted onto the streets of New York City with a new warmth in his heart. He was wide-eyed as he craned his neck to see the top of the New York City skyline, with the buildings all five or six stories high. The other children as well as the ladies remained speechless as they, too, focused on their new "modern" surroundings.

"Let's take the women and children to the hotel, and then we'll see if we can find the trunks, Conrad," Christian suggested. "We'll hope that they are still at the cargo company." Conrad nodded as he pulled the addresses and map from his pocket.

Located in "Kleindeutschland" — little Germany — the hotel was one of the many monotonous brownstone dwellings on First Avenue. There in "Kleindeutschland," life, language, and customs differed greatly from the rest of New York City. One needn't even know English to survive — German was the only language spoken, making it a desirable place for immigrants to reside.

Walking through the streets, structures towered over them and blocked the upcoming sun as the family searched for First Avenue and got their first taste of New York City. Livelier, bigger, and dirtier than Hanover, Berlin, or Bremen, some of the passing carriages sank up to their axles in the mud. Awestruck by all of the sights, the Pollmanns decided that they could only have found such structures and monuments in Europe if they had visited Paris, London, or Rome.

Walking through the crowded boulevards and dark, muddy alleys, they finally found the Hotel Berlin, and they clamored up the worn, stone steps. It was also constructed of brownstone, four stories high. Comforters hung out the open windows, being aired just as in Germany. The ground floor windows had flower boxes covering their sills with newly planted red geraniums sporting green leaves through the black soil. It was now nearly noon, and already the smell of sauerkraut penetrated the air as they opened the large wooden door to the reception area.

The German clerk was gracious, speaking with a Berlin accent. Short and husky with graying at the temples, the middle-aged gentleman helped the weary travelers up the three flights of stairs to their rooms. Small but clean, the bedroom contained a bed, dresser, sink, and closet, and the family rejoiced at the sight. The toilet facilities and bath were shared by the entire floor, but this was a custom they accepted in Europe. Privacy had become something that they didn't have on the ship, and now everything offered in the Hotel Berlin was deemed a luxury to them. It was with restraint that they contained themselves.

As the ladies and children settled in, Christian, Conrad, and Anton made their way through "Kleindeutschland" where every tailor, baker, butcher, and shopkeeper was German. It was easy to understand how immigrants just off the boat wanted to stay with the security of 75,000 Germans, nestled in a small space of the huge, intimidating New York City. It was a clean, neat section in comparison to the filth through which the Pollmanns earlier walked, and it was a temptation too big to pass up for many newcomers.

Fumbling through the streets in search of the American Cargo Company, the three men finally located it near the docks, which harbored the boats going up the Hudson River toward Chicago. The warehouse was huge and the men wondered how anything could be found or labeled with a transfer to another destination. However, they had receipts with numbers, and within half an hour, the trunks were located. Ready to leave on the next day's train for Chicago, the luggage was in a "holding area" near the railway. The Pollmanns immediately realized how lucky they were to still have the trunks in New York City. Christian said a silent prayer of thanks. Because the trunks were heavy, the clerk offered to keep them for a day until the Pollmanns could return. Deciding that clean clothes hardly warranted lugging the trunks across New York City and that the tattered clothes in their rucksacks would suffice for one more night, the three thanked the clerk and agreed to get the trunks the next day before catching their boat going west.

Now close to the docks, the men found a ticket booth selling passages to the Midwest. With no clamoring, pushing lines as in Bremen, they waited only 15 minutes to obtain information about the voyage. They discovered that they could purchase tickets that would take them up the Hudson by boat to the Great Lakes, docking briefly in Chicago before traveling down the Illinois River to Pekin. Anton, Lena, Isabella, and Edith would depart at Chicago, taking a wagon toward northern Indiana.

Christian retrieved the money from the hidden pouch still tied around his leg, astonished to find that he had just enough to pay for the 14 tickets that would give them passage to the Midwest. The thought crossed his mind that the good Lord had placed some extra coins in the pouch, as he was sure that he would come up short. Again, he said a silent prayer of thanks. With his pouch empty, they would all have to rely on Conrad for funds, which Louisa had hidden in the hem of her dress. Conrad would put the money into a pouch that he would tie with a leather strap around his waist.

Christian clutched the tickets in his hand as they quickly rounded a corner, and Conrad then placed them into his secret pocket. Wanting to be safe, the men realized that pick pocketing was an affluent business in America's large cities as well as in Europe's.

The ladies and children were in a joyous mood when the men returned. Having found new friends in the nearby tenements with whom to play, the children were elated to run in the streets after two months of being restricted on the ship. The Pollmann ladies chatted merrily to the mothers and housewives sitting on the stoops, as they watched their children play.

"Papa, this is Minnie," said little Margaretha as Christian approached. "She lives there in that house." Margaretha pointed to a brownstone tenement building, neatly adorn with freshly painted white flower boxes at every window. "Can she come with us to Illinois?"

"I'm afraid not, darling. She'd miss her ma and pa," Christian replied, patting the blonde curls of the little girl with the large sparkling blue eyes. Hardly hearing the answer, the two children giggled as they hugged each other and grabbed their dolls and returned to their tea party.

It was a joyous day for all. It was the first firm soil their feet had touched in over two months. Although the new city was intimidating with immense buildings and commotion of traffic and people in the streets, it was comforting to be in an area — if only for one night — that was comprised of no one but Germans. The ladies laughed and exchanged stories of their children while the men asked detailed questions of travel, work, and life in general in the New World.

* * * * *

By 6 o'clock, the hotel had prepared a wonderful meal for the travelers — pea soup, bread, and potato pancakes. The Pollmanns ate their first official meal together in America around a large round oak table, adorned with an ivory lace tablecloth.

The feather beds were a luxury all had forgotten as they crawled in at 10 o'clock for a night's sleep. It rained that night and hearing the patter on the roof and against the windows were sounds that Christian loved. Always yearning to stay in bed when it rained, he had missed hearing those familiar sounds. He lay with Elizabeth in his arms — she was now twelve weeks pregnant with a definite bulge — as he heard the children still giggling in the nearby beds. All eight of them had been put into four small beds in Christian and Elizabeth's room. It was the only bedroom large enough to accommodate extra beds, so the seven children slumbered together yet another night. Tucked into the center of all the children was Jurgen, who was definitely now a part of the family. To the children, it seemed he had always been a Pollmann.

"Children, you need to sleep. It's a long day tomorrow," Christian whispered. Temporarily, they hushed but long after 11 o'clock, he still heard a giggle escape from Margaretha's lips.

"Let them be, Chris," Elizabeth said. "The first night in the New World will only happen once. Right now they are carefree of all problems. Soon enough we'll all be faced with trials, and even the children will be affected."

By midnight everyone lay in a deep slumber. The children laid curled together in the their beds, legs and arms flung across each other. Louisa, Lena, Conrad, Regina, and baby Maria occupied an adjacent room with a connecting door. Anton, his sister, and cousin stayed in a room down the hall. It was a happy night — one about which the Pollmanns often spoke in the coming years. Christian ended his prayers that night with a special thanks to his Lord for safe passage to America and for all of the lives of his family who arrived unharmed onto the shores of the New World. For that moment, peace, hope, and serenity resided in all of their lives and hearts, helping them to focus on the upcoming journey through life, soon to be filled with new experiences beyond all expectations.

Twenty-six

MARCUS

May 7 — the first morning in the New World — dawned early for Christian Pollmann. Fog and drizzle clouded the sun's visibility from the world of taverns, markets, and boarding houses in the gluttonous New York City. Christian stood at the window and was dressed in a clean nightshirt given him by Frau Whrel who managed the Hotel Berlin. He watched teams of horses already pulling brewery wagons through the streets, filled with brown puddles, a reminder of the night's rain. The gaslights — glowing gold in the fog and mist — lined the narrow streets, flanked by buildings, and the lights illuminated the butcher's shop across the way. Fleshly slaughtered geese and rabbits hung at the door, and signs of "butter 30 cents a pound and coffee 21 cents" showed through the dimly lit window.

"Christian," Elizabeth whispered as she rose onto one elbow with strands of long dark hair falling over her sleepy brown eyes. "Come back to bed, darling. It's so early."

Her olive skin seemed pale, and Christian wondered if it was because of the dim morning's light or because of the long, tedious days of journeying.

"I can't sleep, Elizabeth. I'm going to dress and walk through the streets. I want a look at the New World in the early morning even if it's foggy."

Hurriedly, Christian dressed, slipping out of the room and into the hall, which was lit by a single gaslight near the stairs. Pulling on his well-worn jacket, Christian stepped onto the streets of New York. As he strolled through "Kleindeutschland" and entered a side alley, Christian noticed that the streets were clean just as in Germany, but many of the apartment buildings in this area seemed shabby, his first reminder that he was in America and not his homeland. Because the landlords knew that many of the immigrant Germans would not leave their beloved "Kleindeutschland," they seldom considered improving the living conditions. The crowded German tenants paid their rent on time, kept the buildings and area clean, and never complained. The greedy landlords grew wealthier as the German immigrants continued to fill the already crowded "Kleindeutschland."

A café was already open, serving not only eggs and sausage but also brats and onions. The small room filled with round tables and chairs plus a dining bar with tall stools was overrun with Germans, all chattering about local happenings. Christian took a seat on a bar stool near the window. A unique experience for him, the tall stool was something he hadn't seen, and he slid over the round seat, letting his long legs fall until his feet touched the floor. Perched high, Christian watched the street activities.

He ordered coffee and listened to the men at the nearby table talk of the dingy, dirty factory that they called home for 12 hours each day. Apparently just getting off work, the two stopped for a brat and beer before heading home to see their children who would be leaving for school.

Half-listening to the conversation, Christian peered out the window to the still-hazy morning. Focusing on the passersby, all dressed in work clothes suitable for the factory, Christian's eyes fell on a familiar face. Piercing eyes, black unkempt beard, and faded shirt with slouch hat, he recognized the man as the informant telling of Ignatius' murder. He hadn't changed — same clothes with the exact look in his eyes that previously caused a surge of suspicion in Christian.

He watched the ruffian as he stopped to converse with a gentleman who looked out of place in "Kleindeutschland." He had an affluent appearance — dark business suit with black polished shoes and white shirt. The conversation was brief and with a quick handshake, they departed. The man from the ship lingered near the building across the street, trying to avoid the splashes of muddy water from the brewery wagons.

"Excuse me," Christian said as he turned to the two gentlemen who were enjoying a second cup of strong German coffee after their breakfast. "The man standing across the street — do you know him?"

One man, dressed in a faded brown work shirt and busily stirring his coffee, glanced out the window. "No, can't say that I do."

The other gentleman peered over this rimmed glasses. Obviously somewhat educated, he was reading the morning German newspaper. "I don't know him, but I saw him in here last night. Name is Marcus, I think. Do you know him?"

"He was on the *Don Quixote*, coming from Germany. We arrived yesterday," Christian replied. "But, no, I don't really know him."

"Strange that he came from Germany," the man answered as he folded the newspaper and removed his glasses. "He spoke French in here with the gentleman he was sitting with. Spoke German, too, but with a slight accent. Another man joined him at his table, and that's when I heard his name. Not many Frenchmen in this area, so he stood out, you know."

"Let's go, Max," the gentleman in the faded work shirt said as he finished his coffee. "Getting late."

"Yes, it is," Max replied, checking the clock on the wall. It was 7:30. "Good morning to you," he said, tipping his cap to Christian as he rose.

"Good morning, sirs," Christian answered, nodding his head in a respectful reply.

A glance out the window told Christian that Marcus had disappeared. Finishing his coffee, Christian reached into his pocket, embarrassed as he realized that he had no American money. Dropping some German coins onto the table, he left the crowded café.

* * * * *

Inside the hotel, the rooms came alive as the children awoke to discover their first day in the New World. Excited, they peered out the window at the cloud-covered sky and the rows of tall buildings flanking the narrow streets of the city.

"May I go see Minnie?" Margaretha asked. "I want to play with her."

"No, honey," replied Elizabeth. "We need to get ready to leave on the boat."

"We just got off the boat," little Karl inserted. "I don't want to leave here."

"We're going to see your pa, Karl. We can't see him if we stay here," Elizabeth replied. "Now, you children wash because we're going to eat soon. We need to be at the dock at 10 o'clock."

Hurriedly, the children washed — older ones helping the younger ones — as the ladies straightened the rooms and quickly packed their meager belongings into their rucksacks. Christian had meanwhile snuck into the room, scooping up the children — one by one — from the bed. Their cleanly scrubbed faces beamed as he told them about the New World in the early morning hours. They giggled as Chris described the fairy dust that was falling from the sky, making it foggy and difficult to see.

"The fairy dust is everywhere except at the top of the tall buildings. Up there you can see the golden sun," Christian continued. He looked at the girls whose eyes were wide and twinkling. "Red birds are flying in the blue sky high above the buildings." Christian waved his hands above his head, showing how the birds were flying in the heavens. Margaretha and Elise whispered to each other, trying to imagine the unbelievable scene as Mary questioned the entire scenario.

Chris laughed, winking to the girls so they realized he was teasing, and his mind wandered back to the café and Marcus. He reminded himself that he was leaving Marcus and the murder of Ignatius behind, as the Pollmanns would be leaving for the Midwest in a matter of hours. Still, Christian wondered if Marcus knew who killed Ignatius. Was he himself the murderer? The mystery would remain unsolved for Christian — or so he thought.

Twenty-seven

ON THE *JULIA BELLE*

Eyes were again turned skyward towards the buildings as the family made their trek across New York City to the docks. They had walked these city streets the day before as tired, overwhelmed, and lost immigrants. Today, with a fresh look on life, they gawked again at the huge structures, this time not as awestruck but with renewed interest as to how such buildings could have been built.

Here and there, golden rays sprinkled the streets, but mostly the buildings blocked the sun, and shadows engulfed the inner city. It was cool and windy as the Pollmanns hustled toward the docks located blocks away. Occasionally, one of the adults ducked into a small grocery store, grabbing an item or two advertised on an outdoor sign and dropping their newly acquired American coins onto the counter. Stuffing food into their rucksacks, they prepared for the journey up the Hudson.

It was 1852, and people were just beginning to experience steamboats as a means of travel. Prior to now, steamboats were used only commercially to transport furs, lead, and supplies for forts. As the boats improved and became more plentiful, however, it became feasible for immigrants moving west to employ them.

Water travel with children was safer and easier than with wagons over the treacherous land routes. Now families could move together with speed and relative safety rather than waiting for the father to make the arduous venture alone through the wilderness with hopes of his returning for his family months later. For the first time in history, the settlers no longer had to depend on beasts of burden and their own brute muscle strength to painstakingly move over the hazardous mountains and through the deep ravines. In addition, attacks by Indians and packs of wild animals were lessened with river travel, and now impossible speeds of eight miles an hour allowed immigrants to move in mass toward the Midwest.

Hiring a wagon to carry their trunks a short distance from the American Cargo Company to the docks, the Pollmanns found passage on the *Julia Belle*, which was heading up the Hudson, bound for Chicago. Made of pine, the *Julia Belle* was already packed with grocery items, parcels, clothing, and wheat. With a paddle wheel that could turn up to 20 times a minute, the boat was powered by a coal engine. Captain Benjamin Clements piloted the *Julia Belle*. A large burly man with bushy white sideburns that extended down into his full beard, he had a reputation of being punctual, fair, and decent. The crew was devoted to him, and passengers enjoyed his company when he had time to socialize.

The *Julia Belle* left promptly on time — 11 o'clock. Traveling 90-100 miles each day, they were scheduled to dock in Chicago on May 18. Each evening promptly at 6 o'clock, the boat docked in a harbor. Passengers could either go ashore to find refuge in a hotel or stay aboard, sleeping on pallets on one of the two decks. Farmers were always waiting at the docks, selling produce cheaply. Passengers would buy enough food to last until the next evening when the process would be repeated. In every village, early spring apples, cheese, fresh bread, milk, and dried meat were offered by the farmers. On occasion, some of the travelers would dine at a local restaurant, eating freshly caught sturgeon, shad, or oysters.

The Hudson River flowed upward through the deep purple ravines and green sloping hillsides of the Hudson Highlands and through the picturesque Catskill Mountains. Travel through this majestic landscape gave the passengers an opportunity to view the icy cold waters flanked on both sides by lush green forests. The travelers were in awe as the beauty and incredible wonder of the great river unfolded at every bend. On the first day, people stood on the deck watching the villages pass — Nyack, Croton, Peekstill, Bear Mountain, Cold Spring, and Cornwall. Castles, historic mansions, century-old lighthouses, spiraling cliffs, sandy beaches, and rolling hills could all be seen from the *Julia Belle*, and the immigrants wondered if all of America was just as spectacular as the New England area.

The second day on the steamboat, the passengers realized that river travel — although faster and safer than wagon trains — also held dangers in its currents. Because the Hudson River actually flowed both ways, the Indians had named it *Muheakantuck* (river flowing both ways). Thus, because of the dynamics of the currents, changes could come quickly, with such occurrences as flooding or erosion from the shoreline. Where water was once deep, it could suddenly be shallow with hidden debris capable of sinking a boat.

The passengers experienced first-hand just such a treacherous circumstance when two days into the trip, Captain Clements was piloting the boat and rounding a bend when — without warning — erosion loomed in front. Back-paddling sent some passengers flying as the Captain attempted to stop the *Julia Belle*, redirecting her onto a different route around the bend. Undoubtedly, Clement's quick thinking kept the steamboat from being beached and frightened passengers quickly realized the difficulties of river travel.

Erosion deposits were not the only hazards. It was not unusual for steamboat smoke stacks to be damaged by large, overhanging tree branches or hulls to be punctured by snags that didn't exist on the previous journey. On the fourth afternoon of the journey, near Quebec, an unseen snag ripped a hole in the hull. Captain Clements and his crew pulled ashore as the travelers disembarked onto the banks. For four hours, the crew worked while the passengers told stories, lay in the warm spring sun, or gathered wild berries. The children ran through the meadows as mothers stayed nearby watching for wild animals or Indians. Although it was great fun for the youngsters, the adults were relieved when the boat had been repaired. Horror stories had circulated of irreparable boats that were abandoned for a different steamboat or worse yet, a wagon train to carry the travelers to their destination.

It was during this incident that Christian saw his first Native American. As the children played in the meadow, plush with tall grass and sprinkled with yellow buttercups, Christian walked to the top of the hill overlooking a vast valley. There, situated on the flat plain was an array of tepees. Staring for a few moments unsure of what they were, Christian saw thin circles of smoke spiraling through the tops of the odd-shaped structures. As he focused on the tepees, two riders approached from the nearby forest. Dark-skinned men with long black braids falling down their naked backs, they sat astride spotted ponies. Attired in breechclouts, the two dismounted.

Christian caught sight of still other men, partially hidden from view, wearing their full headdress of feathers. Suspicions were now confirmed — he was getting his first glimpse of Native Americans, and he glanced over his shoulder to check on the children. Still playing in the grass, he again turned his attention to the valley below. The Indians were retreating into the largest tepee, and in a matter of seconds, all that was left in the distance were the ponies and the strange structures with thin spirals of smoke circling into the sky. Before they arrived in Chicago, they would see tribes of Iroquois, Mohican, Mohawk, Chippewa, and Kickapoo. Complex, strange people that he now feared, Christian would eventually learn to respect and love the Native American.

Twenty-eight

MARCUS RESURFACES

For the first time since the Pollmanns left Germany, language became a barrier. Aboard the *Don Quixote* and in "Kleindeutschland," everyone spoke German — most passengers who left from Bremerhaven were German, and, of course, "Kleindeutschland" was exclusively German. Now, as they left these safe havens, English predominated. Christian and Conrad spoke a little English, and Anton was quite fluent. Trying to teach the children one word at a time, Anton started with the basics — spoon, fork, tree, river, boat, bird, and sky were their first words. By the end of the fourth day, the children knew a slew of words, and they sat on deck — under the bright noonday sun — giggling and practicing their new-found language. As one of the girls would run to Anton to grasp a new word, she would return to her cousins to introduce it, making them guess the German meaning. When they grew tired of playing this game, they turned to their marbles or blocks of colored wood, which Conrad had purchased at one of the stops. Everything was new and interesting, and the children were too overwhelmed and thrilled with life to be homesick for Hummersen.

Elizabeth, however, was not feeling the same excitement as the children. Tired, sometimes nauseated, and utterly confused, she yearned for the normalcy of home. She longed for her own bed, the old fireplace on which to cook a "real" meal, her garden, and most of all, her parents. Also, at this point, she wanted the security of knowing Olga, the local midwife, would help deliver her baby, due in December. Trying to hide her feelings from her husband, she cried softly after he was asleep.

Elizabeth tried to occupy her days by watching the incredible scenery. Hundreds of buffalo roamed the flatland, and antelope, moose, and elk were bountiful in the northern parts of the country. The gray wolf ran in packs, and the bobcat and lynx dotted the edges of the river as they emerged from the forest for a drink. Graceful, beautiful, and agile, the animals watched with curiosity as the steamboat chugged by.

By the end of the first week, everyone had had his first view of Indians. Some of the Native Americans were gathered on hills while others were near the water's edge, all studying the strange boat floating down the river. The passengers, unwilling to take their eyes off the Native Americans, were interested mostly in their dress. Men in only breechclouts and beaded moccasins and women clothed in long beaded, leather dresses with fringe were a phenomenon to the immigrants. Talking quietly to each other, the travelers absorbed as much as they could as they stared from the distant boat.

Just before the *Julia Belle* entered Lake Huron, a few of the passengers spotted black smudge curling upward, darkening the otherwise clear, blue sky. Too far to distinguish the source of the fire, it grew thicker and darker as the travelers gathered on deck to watch. The following day as the boat docked at Sault Ste Marie, Christian heard the news.

A village — Red Rock — had had trouble with the usually peaceful Chippewa. With a misunderstanding over a load of furs that the whites had traded to the Indians, the Chippewa attacked at night, burning the village and killing all of the residents except a dozen young ladies and a random selection of babies, mostly male. The horrific story was not one that Christian wanted to repeat even to Conrad.

Standing among the few townspeople who were discussing the episode, terror swept through Christian again as he wondered if they had made the proper decision in coming to America. What if his entire family had been in that village, all wiped out without a chance to survive? He thought back about

Elizabeth's friend, Wilhelmina, whose sister, Dorthea, and her children had been massacred. Taking a moment, he thanked the Lord that they were not a part of the Red Rock murders, his family was safe, and his unborn child was well and healthy.

"Many Indians are not vicious, and no one knows of the real misunderstanding that took place there," one of the townspeople was saying. Pulling himself from the reverie, Christian realized that the man was speaking to him.

"What did you say?" Christian said with a thick accent.

"You looked horrified, and I was saying that not all of the Indians are mean. In fact, local Indians make friends with their white neighbors. Usually, it's the wild bands that come through randomly that we have to fear. That doesn't often happen."

Christian tried to muster a smile as he nodded, understanding only a portion of the conversation. Returning to the steamboat, he was determined to protect the women from the news. Unless someone told the entire story in German, the ladies wouldn't understand enough of the tale told in English to understand. At least that was his hope. When asked about the black smoke, Christian feigned innocence, saying that he couldn't find out and quickly changed the subject.

As the steamboat entered the State of Michigan, on its way to Chicago, many log cabins were visible along Lake Michigan's edge. Built in the midst of evergreens so thick that not a sparkle of sunlight could penetrate, the crude structures were a fascination to the Germans.

"People live there all year?" Anton questioned one of the crew members.

"Oh, yes. It's quite comfortable inside the cabin. One room offers a fireplace, living, dining, and kitchen area," Andrew, one of the crew answered. "They're called log cabins, and the logs are notched together so they fit tightly. Then to seal the cabin from the wind, they chink and daub the cracks with a type of mortar."

Anton's mind was reeling with the information — one room in which to live? Logs for building materials?

Christian interrupted his thoughts. "We'll all get used to the new ways, Anton. You'll have Lena to help you," he smiled.

Silently, Christian had doubts of any quick adaptation himself, but he was resolved to remain positive for the sake of his family.

They stopped that night northeast of Chicago at Muskegon. It was May 17, and they were on schedule. As the boat docked, a rather shabbily dressed gentleman approached Captain Clements, pulling him aside, and Christian strained to see the man's face. His movements and gestures seemed familiar. Many of the passengers were already disembarking, either in search of a hotel for the night or to buy food from vendors. Christian lingered a moment to watch the brief conversation that ensued as the captain sometimes nodded, sometimes shook his head, all the while listening intently. Eventually the poorly dressed man left, but Christian heard "I'll be back in an hour." The captain nodded.

Christian's eyes followed the rag-tag man as he walked away from the captain and descended the gangplank into the crowd of curious onlookers huddled on the dock. In the shadows, a dim light finally fell on a face that Christian knew — Marcus! Looking just as disheveled as before, he had changed from his faded black shirt, but he still sported the black slouch hat and unkempt beard.

Who was this man? Why had he been talking to the captain? First, he was on the *Don Quixote* and disappeared; then he was in New York City and vanished. Now, out of nowhere, he appeared in Michigan. Questions inundated Christian's mind as he stared at the elusive "Marcus."

"What's wrong, Christian?" Conrad, on his way to the gangplank, was stopped by Christian's confused, worried, and rather frightened expression.

"It's the man from the *Don Quixote*," Christian answered, quickly adding, "the one who knew of the murder on board."

Conrad was silent, searching the crowd for a bearded face with dark, piercing eyes.

"He's gone," Christian commented. "I saw him in New York City, too."

With raised eyebrows, Conrad responded, "New York City? Really? You didn't mention it."

"I know. I really didn't expect to see him again, so I didn't bother to tell you. His name is Marcus," Christian continued, "and he speaks both French and German. Apparently, he speaks English as well. He isn't German, however, because he has an accent. It's all curious since he was on the *Don Quixote*, which carried only Germans."

"How do you know all of this?" Conrad asked.

"Two gentlemen in New York told me. Listen, Conrad, our family is on the dock getting food, and that man is scary."

Conrad nodded and together they quickly joined their wives who were attempting to understand one of the farmer's limited German. Putting a jug of milk, nuts, berries, and bread into their rucksacks, the ladies were delighted with their purchases. Grabbing the bags, the men hustled their families toward the gangplank.

Planning to spend the night on the lower deck, the ladies took the children below to feed them and prepare their pallets. Conrad and Christian took cheese and slices of bread to the upper deck, and they sat in the darkened shadows, waiting for the return of Marcus.

More than an hour passed and the two thought plans had changed when Marcus appeared out of nowhere, quickly disappearing below. Within seconds a stranger scurried by with a stocky Black lady, hair pulled back into a tight bun, fear showing in her dark eyes. Along with her ragged three small children, they all descended the stairwell to some unknown place.

Exchanging glances, Conrad and Christian quickly followed the entourage, not only fearful for their own families below, but also curious about the newcomers. Although they were close behind, by the time the two reached the bottom rung of the staircase, the area was vacated of all people. Bewildered, Christian searched behind the boiler, but it was as if no one at all had preceded them to the lower level.

Still confused by the seemingly paranormal observation, the two joined their wives and children, already lying on pallets in one corner of the boat. Silent but vigilant for the next hour, Christian sat attempting to sort through the situation. Who was the Black lady? Obvious fear showed in her eyes. Were the men taking her and the children hostage? Or maybe they were fugitives. Where could they have gone?

As he sat thinking, he decided that there must be an opening to the bowels of the steamboat. He hadn't seen it, but perhaps that's where the six people had disappeared. It was the only logical explanation. Christian lay awake for some time, wondering if the Captain was harboring fugitives or holding hostages. As he finally started to drift into a fitful sleep, he decided that he might never know the truth of the situation.

Twenty-nine

CHICAGO, ILLINOIS

Christian's sleep was interrupted with sporadic episodes of lying awake thinking of Marcus to thoughts of the Black lady with her children. He awoke at 7 o'clock, more tired than when he had gone to sleep. Slipping from his pallet, he went above board for fresh air. Not wanting to stray far from his family, he stood, looking out over the town of Muskegan. The rutted streets, already crowded with early morning wagons loaded with produce, were wet from a night's rain. Farmers — dressed in overalls and boots — waded through the mud to set up market.

"Christian," Elizabeth called from below, "could you see if the farmers have more fresh milk? The children drank most of what we bought last night."

Elizabeth had felt Christian leave the warmth of his pallet, and with tired eyes, she visually followed him up the stairs. Knowing he had seemed preoccupied for days, she had hoped her husband would share his problems. All too often, though, he kept his worries to himself so as not to trouble her.

As Chris expected upon returning to the lower level, there still was no sign of the stranger, and during breakfast, he and Conrad exchanged silent glances on several occasions. As usual, 8 o'clock was the time set to sail — the last day on the *Julia Belle*. Arriving in Chicago, they would board a different steamboat and precede on the last leg of their journey — down the Illinois River to Tazewell County and their final destination, Pekin.

* * * * *

As they proceeded south into northern Illinois, the rolling hills gave way to wide, open prairies, skirted by thick forests. The young spring grass swayed under the warm May sun, and blue, yellow, and violet flowers were beginning to carpet parts of the flat land. The travelers all stood on deck, absorbing their first view of northern Illinois, and by late afternoon, Chicago could be seen in the distance. Located on the edge of the beautiful blue Lake Michigan, it was the Midwest's largest inland port.

Only recently had the Illinois and Michigan canal connected Chicago to downstate Illinois, making inland travel much more easy and feasible. The city of Chicago, consisting of 30,000 inhabitants, was definitely the largest settlement in the Midwest and growing with leaps and bounds. And with the opening of the canal in 1848, hundreds of pioneers were moving to the prairie state in search of farm land, water resources, and a new way of life.

As the *Julia Belle* docked in the harbor, the passengers were glued to the sights. Chicago was sprawled out along Lake Michigan with row after row of light-colored five- and six-story limestone buildings, all fringing the narrow streets. Theaters, churches, and commercial buildings could all be seen from the deck of the *Julia Belle* as passengers started to disembark, retrieving their trunks, which were being placed on the dock by the crew.

Unsure of what to do next, Christian suggested that he search for a place to stay while the rest waited on the dock. The children — again overjoyed to be free of the confines of the boat — ran helter- skelter along the dock and onto the sandy beach, with Anton and Lena close behind. Hundreds of people, who were enjoying the golden Illinois sun, walked along the beach or swam in the crystal blue Lake Michigan.

Gone about an hour, Christian returned with good and bad news. Cheaper hotels were all filled, leaving them with no room accommodations except for expensive ones on Michigan Boulevard. The good news was they did have a place to stay — free!

Upon going into the Trinity Church on Jackson Street to rest momentarily, gather his thoughts, and offer a brief prayer for guidance, Christian met the pastor, who was at the altar arranging flowers for the weekend services. Being for the first time in over two months in a church, Christian approached the reverend, asking for communion. Unable to take proper sacraments during the time on the boat, Christian wished to have bread broken for him.

Amazingly, the pastor was a German Lutheran and originally from Hanover, near Hummersen. Christian kneeled on the communion bench at the front of the humble church. The altar was simply dressed in purple vestments and a single stained glass window adorned the area behind the cross. Most of the windows on the sides of the sanctuary were leaded glass, sprinkled with Biblical pictures done in various colors of blue, red, and green stained glass. Definitely not elaborate, the church was warm and inviting, and Christian felt at home even as he knelt for communion.

After receiving bread and wine, Christian engaged the pastor in conversation, asking for directions to a hotel that was clean and reasonably priced. Without hesitation, the reverend invited Christian to bring his family to the church. It was warm, clean, and safe.

"So we're staying in the church?" Elise asked as Christian finished his story.

"Yes, Pastor Wieburg said we could stay as long as necessary," Christian smiled.

"That's perfect," Elizabeth replied as she breathed a long sigh of relief. Obviously tired, her pregnancy weighing on her, she was glad for a night's refuge.

Regina, too, looked pale, exhausted. Eight-month-old Maria had been fussy for several days. With swollen gums and a dripping nose, Regina knew she was attempting to cut a tooth.

It was then that Christian saw Conrad in the distance. He was engaged in conversation with a man and young boy who Christian had seen aboard the *Don Quixote*. Talking with them on several occasions on the way from Germany, Conrad had told Christian that they were very poor and destitute. They had worked for two years to get enough money for boat passage and were headed for

St. Louis. Not having been on the *Julia Belle*, the two must have found another boat coming to Chicago. Chris wondered where they had attained the money since their entire savings had been used for passage to New York City. They were trailing along with Conrad as he approached Christian.

"Chris, do you remember Nicholaas and Herman from Berlin?" Conrad asked.

"Yes, of course," Christian responded, extending his hand to both. "You're headed for St. Louis, right?"

"Yes, we are," the man answered.

"They have no place to stay tonight. Did you find a room for us, Christian?" Conrad questioned.

"Actually, we're staying in a church not far from here." He hesitated for a moment, then added, "I'm sure it would be all right for Herman and Nicholaas to join us."

Herman again extended his hand to Chris in a gesture of thanks. "That's very kind of you, sir. We promise to be no trouble."

The two were obviously grateful, and Christian's heart always went out to the poor, feeling an inner warmth when he could be of help. However, there was something about these two that he didn't like. Unable to put his finger on it, he chided himself for having negative feelings about the two Germans who were destitute. After all, Nicholaas was only a boy — perhaps 13. He seemed a strange lad, always silent with downcast eyes. Perhaps, he was deaf, Christian thought. Remarkably, though, Conrad seemed to like and trust both of them because he had talked with them on previous occasions. So what was it about them that made Christian feel uneasy? He didn't know and made an attempt to brush the thought aside.

Mustering a smile, Christian nodded to Herman. "It will be no problem."

"Chris," Conrad interrupted, "I have our steamboat booked — *The Delta Queen*. We leave tomorrow at 10 o'clock in the morning, traveling south through the state on the Illinois River. We should arrive the next night in Pekin."

Christian suddenly realized that their journey was nearly complete, and a reunion with his brother was only a day away. Amazing that two months ago,

Fredrich was thousands of miles away, and now he was a mere 180 miles from where the Pollmanns stood. It was an incredible feat in 1852.

Not only was Fredrich near but also "home" was within reach. No wonder the children were in a tither, racing up and down the dock. There would be no more living from a rucksack or being imprisoned in a berth below deck. Soon, they would all have beds on which to sleep, land to farm, and a house — no matter how meager — to call their own. And along with all of this would come new people with whom they could form lasting friendships and a church to help build a foundation. It would be a new, different way of life, but at least they would possess a sense of stability with a daily routine.

Christian's thoughts were interrupted by Anton who was calling to Lena. As he raced toward them, he waved something in his hand.

"Lena, Lena, I've got the tickets," he cried.

Momentarily, Christian had forgotten that it was here that Lena, Anton, Isabella and Edith would be departing for Indiana.

"We'll have to stay in Chicago for two nights," Anton said, out of breath, "but we sail for Gary, Indiana, on Monday morning."

Christian knew from the look on the Haas sisters' faces that they dreaded the moment of separation, but a new life laid ahead for all of them. Through their inner strength, which God provided, they would succeed.

Flagging down a horse and buggy, they loaded their trunks. Jurgen, although small, proved strong and with a little help, he assisted the men in heaving the loads up onto the buggy. Elizabeth took the only seat available after the luggage had been packed and made the short ride to Trinity Church. The rest of the family walked through the streets of Chicago, again in awe of the buildings — their light-colored limestone, the multitude of numbers, and, of course, the immense height of five to six-stories high. Some streets and sidewalks were paved, something the immigrants hadn't seen. They became the dominant topic of conversation as the Pollmanns made their way to the church.

At that moment, no one felt the pangs of homesickness. The streets seemed paved with gold and the sky was alive and blue all the way to Heaven. America was everything and more than they had heard when they were still living in Hummersen.

Thirty

CHICAGO TO PEKIN

What better place for the Pollmanns to find refuge than in a Lutheran church. Feeling the need to be quiet in God's house, the children played silently in the Narthex. Having brought blankets and pillows for the visitors, the reverend sat, talked, and prayed with the immigrants until 8 o'clock that night. It was then that the parents proclaimed bedtime for the children. After the youngsters were settled, Pastor Wieburg offered communion to the adults.

Nicholaas and Herman seemed a bit reluctant to take communion, saying they were Catholic but had fallen away from the church during the last years of living in destitute. As the Pollmanns gathered for the sacrament, Nicholaas and Herman retreated from the church into the precarious night streets of Chicago.

It was midnight when Christian still lay awake and heard the two re-enter the church through a side door. Quickly and quietly taking blankets to the other side of the sanctuary, they passed Christian, who detected a whiff of alcohol. Curious as to how homeless, penniless people had money for liquor, Christian was also concerned if young Nicholaas was being led down the woeful path of destruction. Having earlier noticed the lifeless glazed look in Nicholaas' eyes, Christian worried that unproductive ways were already a permanent feature in his lifestyle. Pushing the thought from his mind, he knew he needed to sleep. With Margaretha, Anna-Marie, Jurgen, and now another little Pollmann on the way, Chris had precious little time to worry about a 13-year-old whom he had just met and probably would never see again.

Christian looked at Jurgen lying next to him. The full, bright moon showed through the leaded glass windows, casting shadows onto his small, innocent face. Christian whispered a prayer of thanks that they were able to save the child from destruction and make him part of their family.

As Christian turned over, his thoughts slowly shut down as he fell into a short but sound slumber — so sound that he didn't hear or feel his wife rise from her pallet and creep off into the dimness of the church's sanctuary.

*   *   *   *

Awaking the next morning, Christian heard his wife's voice in the distance, chattering excitedly. Rising onto one elbow, he could see her in the shadows caused by early morning sunlight. She was peeking through the church windows. Standing with her arm around Regina, Elizabeth stood next to Lena and Anton with Isabella and Edith sitting in the nearby pew. Frightened as to why they were up so early and obviously had been for a while, he attempted to decipher the circumstances. Apparently not upset, though, they were laughing and hugging, leaving Christian completely bewildered. Looking over and seeing Christian, Elizabeth motioned for him to join them.

"Chris, meet Mr. and Mrs. Anton Schumacher," Elizabeth said with excitement in her voice.

Lena and Anton stood, hand-in-hand, beaming.

Before he could answer, Elizabeth continued. "They were married early this morning, soon after midnight. After you went to sleep, Lena woke me, asking if I'd join her. With Pastor Wieburg available, it seemed the perfect time for a wedding."

"We're starting our new life today — May 19 — as husband and wife," Lena glowed.

"Well, congratulations," Chris stammered as he shook Anton's hand and took Lena into his arms, kissing both cheeks. "This is wonderful. You should have awakened me."

"Elizabeth stood up for Lena, and my sister stood up for me," Anton commented. "A little unorthodox, but Pastor said it was fine. We thought it'd be a great surprise for everyone this morning."

"And, indeed, it is," commented Regina who now had her arm around Lena in a tight grip.

"We have to part today, and it's a little easer knowing that Lena is Anton's wife, and they're going as newlyweds to start their lives in Indiana," Elizabeth said, tears already sparkling in her eyes.

Conrad was aroused by the stir, and as they told him the news, Christian noticed Nicholaas and Herman already gone from their pallets into the early morning. Again, dislike and suspicion stirred within Christian as he glanced at the children to be sure they were safe. All were still, slumbering as he turned his attention again to the newlyweds and their wedding day.

* * * * *

Somehow, when they boarded *The Delta Queen* a few hours later, Nicholaas and Herman were with them. The two returned to the church shortly before the Pollmanns departed, and, miraculously, they had come up with money for passage as far as Tazewell County. There, they'd find work to pay for their final trip to St. Louis.

The sisters' departure from each other was difficult; the 250 miles between Illinois and Indiana seemed enormous but not insurmountable. It would be possible to visit in a few years. Railroads were available already between the states, and journeys were relatively comfortable for the travelers in the 1850s. Attempting to stifle the tears, the girls hugged, kissed, and promised to write as often as possible. As the steamboat pulled out of the port, Anton, Lena, Isabella, and Edith waved until their family was out of sight.

The Delta Queen seemed large — 130 feet long, 20 feet wide, and held a capacity of 95 tons. Freight was carried in the bowels of the steamboat, and as many as 50 passengers sat comfortably on deck, all traveling to Central Illinois. The immigrants found May to be a perfect time to travel down the Illinois River as they headed south through the massive prairies. The early morning sun reflected its light off the myriad of dewdrops, spread over the tall prairie grasses.

By the end of the summer, the stately green prairie would become yellow and wave in the wind like wheat. By then it would become ripe for the huge prairie fires that devastated the farms, land, wildlife, and families. Chris had heard of the terrifying prairie fires of Illinois from Fredrich. Once the inferno started, farmers often had to launch their own fires to "burn back," attempting to extinguish the huge blaze, which destroyed everything in its path. With breezes flickering the fires into torrent flames, a dark curtain soon would sweep the prairies, extending from earth to heaven. For days, the sun, moon, and stars could be obscured, bringing slow death to all victims and vegetation in its path.

But in May, all was green and lush. Violets and coneflowers carpeted acres of land, and flocks of red-breasted robins, Baltimore orioles, chickadees, and skylarks filled the brilliantly blue Illinois skies. The passengers watched herds of graceful deer bound through the prairie grass, heading for refuge in patches of thick, green forests. It was a glorious land — Illinois in 1852 — and the Pollmanns felt blessed to be a part of this new world, soon to be their home.

Impossible to contain the children now that they were close to Pekin and Fredrich, Christian found it difficult to stifle his own excitement. After so many months of planning, saving, and finally making the trip from Hummersen to Bremerhaven and then across the Atlantic to New York City and on to Chicago, the last leg of the journey now seemed interminable.

At last by late afternoon, *The Delta Queen* arrived in Tazewell County. The final stop for the steamboat was Pekin, before retracing its route back to Chicago. A thriving village of 2,500 people, Pekin was established in 1824 by Jonathan Tharp. Moving from Kingston, Illinois, to Pekin, he built a small log cabin on a high east bank of the river. Finding the Pottawatomi Indians to be friendly, many other members of Tharp's family followed, and even though there was much tribulation with disease and war, the village continued to grow and thrive.

The Delta Queen docked at the lower west edge of downtown Pekin. With the town built on a hill above the Illinois River, the passengers on the steamboat could see only the dock, but the Pollmanns were overwhelmed with excitement as their trunks were lifted from the boat's deck and put onto the solid ground of their new hometown.

Thirty-one

LIFE IN PEKIN

Louisa had sent a telegraph to Fredrich from New York City, but at the time she, of course, wasn't sure of their date of arrival in Pekin — she had estimated somewhere between May 18 and May 22. It was late afternoon of May 19 and the sun was starting to dip into the western sky as *The Delta Queen* reached the harbor of Pekin. Partially covered by the tall trees on the opposite bank of the Illinois River, the sun cast golden shadows into the clear waters. A multitude of colorful fish surfaced, creating bubbles and ripples in the otherwise still, placid channel.

With the boat docked, the gangplank was let down. Suddenly hearing a commotion from the children, Louisa turned to find Fredrich, who had already scooped Elise and Karl into his arms. He bent to receive a face full of kisses from Mary as they laughed and cried all at once. Louisa stood watching, unable to move, simply looking at her husband so dearly missed for two years. The moment she had awaited was finally here, and she was too overwhelmed to comprehend.

Amidst the flurry with his children, Fredrich glanced over to find his wife's eyes. He smiled, staring relentlessly into her deep blue chasms as he let his children believe they were getting his undivided attention. Before he could move, his nieces and nephews threw themselves at him and the excitement started over once more. It was a grand reunion for the Pollmann children, and when at last they had had their temporary fill, Fredrich walked slowly toward Louisa, whose face was now wet with tears. Taking her in his arms, he kissed her tenderly and held her close in an embrace which showed the loneliness that he had felt for two years.

"How did you know we were on this boat?" Louisa whispered as Fredrich wiped tears from his wife's face.

"I've met every boat coming from Chicago since yesterday morning. Eventually, I knew you'd be on one," he said with a broad smile. "I was standing behind a tree, and I saw all of you looking out over the railing. I was sure that if I would be quick, I could surprise all of you once the gangplank was let down."

"Well, it worked," Louisa said as she kissed and hugged her husband again.

Chris and Conrad extended manly hugs rather than handshakes as Fredrich's sisters-in-law planted kisses on both of his cheeks. Young Jurgen was introduced as the newest family member, and he beamed as he met his Uncle Fredrich. The joy and excitement were unsurpassed on that May afternoon as Fredrich loaded the trunks onto his wagon. As the children skipped alongside, the Pollmanns went up the hill onto Main Street to view for the first time their new surroundings.

* * * * *

Dozens of horses pulled buggies through the dirt streets that ran down the center of Pekin. Two-story, red brick buildings lined the main road running east and west through the thriving river town that continued to grow because of growing steamboat and ferry trade. Already located on the main drag of the city were several lawyers, doctors, a post office, courthouse, newspaper office, multiple dry good stores, and two saloons. Near the center of town were multiple churches, a school, three small grocery stores, a number of shops manufacturing specified farm materials, and three small warehouses. Pekin seemed to be on its way to a promising future, and Fredrich was anxious to introduce his family to his town in the Midwest.

As they passed the second of the town's two saloons, Christian looked up to see a familiar face peering from the open tavern door. Marcus! In disbelief, Christian looked at the shabbily bearded man with slouch hat and tattered clothes. How could he appear again? First on the *Don Quixote*, then in New York City, then Chicago, and now in Pekin.

Quickly, Christian touched Fredrich's arm. "Fredrich, who is that man standing in the doorway?"

Fredrich followed the direction of Christian's gaze, seeing the rag-tag man at the saloon door. "I don't know. I saw him several days ago at the dry goods store and then again yesterday as I waited at the dock, hoping all of you would be on the steamboat. Actually, I saw him twice at the river. I thought he was waiting for someone."

"He came over on the *Don Quixote*," Chris commented. "I only know that his name is Marcus."

"Really? He came from Germany? I don't think he's German, though," Fredrich inserted. "I heard him speaking to some other Germans at the river, and he has an accent."

"Yes, I know he's not German. I'm not sure of his nationality, but he's a mystery that I plan to solve," Christian replied.

Marcus' nationality and identity were not the only mysteries to Christian. Just as puzzling was how he arrived in Pekin several days before the Pollmanns. Silently, Chris pondered the enigma, trying to put together the pieces, which continually fell into disarray. There didn't seem to be any feasible answers. And then there were Nicholaas and Herman. What had happened to them? In the hubbub of finding Fredrich, they had been forgotten. Actually, somewhat relieved at their disappearance, Christian would have to ask Conrad later.

＊　＊　＊　＊　＊

Fredrich had bought a small farm of 20 acres on the near outskirts on the north side of town. A small house occupied the southeast corner of the land, and Fredrich — with the help of his neighbors — had added a loft for the children. He had worked on cleaning the barn and making it suitable for

Conrad and Christian's families until they could find a place to live, and his German neighbors had cooked enough food for the Pollmanns to feast on for days.

Mainly a community of German immigrants, both the English and German languages could be heard in all stores, churches, and schools. In fact, on a daily basis, it was almost more common to hear German spoken than English. Concerned about the language barrier, Christian asked Fredrich if speaking German would be a problem until they learned English well enough to be fluent. Fredrich shook his head as he reminisced about a story he heard the first week he arrived in Tazewell County.

It happened one day at a grocery store in downtown Pekin. A stranger and his family came through Pekin on their way west. Leaving his wife and children in the hotel, the gentleman walked to the store. Shop owner, Adolph Zieghorst, spoke little English, and the customers in the store at the time spoke only German. The stranger felt as if he had entered a foreign country as he tried to communicate what he needed. Soap and candy were easily understood, but herbs for abdominal cramps for his wife presented a different problem. Finally, after several futile attempts, he left, shaking his head. America as the "melting pot" took on a new meaning that day to the stranger. He said to his wife, "Where else could you enter a grocery store in your own country, speak English, and not be understood! Where else, I say, than in America!"

Fredrich had heard that story from his cousin, Christopher Pollmann, who had come from Hanover and immigrated to Pekin in 1848. Settling in a boarding house near the town's center, he worked as a shoemaker. Christopher introduced Fredrich to many people, found him a place to stay, and helped him land a job. In fact, Fredrich took two jobs within the first month. He worked as a hired hand on a farm during the day, and when the shoemaker's shop closed in late afternoon, Fredrich helped Christopher by candlelight into the late evening, repairing and making shoes.

Packing a small savings aside each month, by the end of the first year, Fredrich had enough money to make a down payment on a farm. Because the owner had died, the farm was sold with the inclusion of all the farm equipment. Fredrich felt lucky to have been at the right place at the right time. Of course, he believed that it wasn't really luck but rather God's hand that had allowed the circumstances to occur.

As with all of the other Pollmanns, religion was an important aspect of Fredrich's life. Joining the Lutheran community when he arrived helped Fredrich establish his religious roots in Pekin. Still meeting in members' homes and in a store on Main Street, St. Johannes Lutheran Church was in the very early stages of development in 1852 with Reverend Mettfeldt from Hamburg leading the congregation.

Even as the church was taking root, there were disagreements among the members. Some of the men were pondering a split from the Lutheran denomination, and Fredrich was one of them. Because he had been raised in the Evangelical Church of Prussia in Falkenhagen, Fredrich and other Germans of similar background were not able to accept some of the stringent Lutheran doctrines. Even though there already were Methodist and Baptist churches in Pekin, many Germans' beliefs didn't fit any of the orthodox American denominations. The pressures of the modern Evangelical reforms learned in Germany under the government of 1817 were in contention with the Lutheran church's strong, rigid sanctions. Fredrich was about to proclaim his independence from St. Johannes Lutheran Church, and he hoped that his brother would follow.

Thirty-two

UNCOVERING THE STORY OF MARCUS

The first days of life in Pekin for the Pollmanns were both fantastic and confusing. Being re-united with Fredrich was incredible for everyone, making Christian wonder how his brother had managed as a new immigrant when he arrived in Pekin with support only from a cousin he barely knew. Community life bewildered the newcomers. There was no time to sit over 10 o'clock morning coffee — as was the custom in Germany — to discuss the day's plans. Work was laborious and demanding in the New World, allowing little opportunity for breaks. Even the evenings often were not spent as family time; chores lasted long into the night. With bills to pay, loans to eradicate, and food to put on the table, the American farmers had to be strong, durable, and resolute.

"I remember your saying that you had never worked so hard as when you moved to America," Christian remarked one early morning as he and Fredrich milked the cows. "I'm only now comprehending that statement," he smiled.

"It's hard work but rewarding. I guess you can say that I'm still working two jobs just as when I first came to America because when weather doesn't permit me to be in the fields, I do carpentry work in town. With hard work, I can save money, and truly I have to say that after two years, I love the American way of life. I wouldn't return to Germany, Chris."

Christian hoped he felt the same way in two years. Right now, he knew that Elizabeth was especially homesick although she didn't admit it, and the children longed for their own beds back in Hummersen, their friends, their dog, and security.

Within the first week, Christian and Conrad both found boarding rooms for lodging. Christian helped Fredrich on the farm but was in search of a cabinet-making occupation while Conrad found work in Weghorst's Shoe Shop with Christopher. Within the second week, Christian had a job at Stein's Cabinet Store, which allowed him to work at the shop during the day and still assist Fredrich in the evenings.

It was at the end of the third week that the Pollmanns gathered at Fredrich and Louisa's home after church for a family meal and camaraderie. With food being prepared by the ladies, Fredrich and Christian went to the living room to talk while Conrad chose to take the children outside to play. Christian saw the weekly newspaper lying on the table and picked it up to peruse the headlines. Part in English and the rest in German, the picture on the front page jumped out at Christian — Nicholaas and Herman in handcuffs with Marcus standing guard.

Collapsing into the chair, wide-eyed, Christian said, "Well, look at this." The article was written in English so Christian handed the paper to Fredrich. "Could you read this to me?"

Fredrich looked at the headlines first, reading, "'Two Renegades Found Hiding in Pekin.'" Fredrich continued, "The article states, 'For over a month, the federal officials have been investigating the murder of a first-class passenger from Germany aboard the *Don Quixote* and thought that these two scoundrels were involved. John Adlehorn, sometimes known as Marcus le Beau, was in Hanover, Germany, on a job for the American federal government when — upon his return to America — he encountered the murder of Ignatius Feltman, who was found dead in his berth on the *Don Quixote*. Since the discovery of the body, Adlehorn had been tracking the murderers. Clues led him to believe that Nicholaas Tapmann and Herman Isenburg were involved, and Adlehorn followed them from New York City to Chicago to Pekin, all the time piecing together evidence. Apparently, Tapmann — only

13 years of age — and Isenburg together murdered Feltman at the request of Feltman's brother, Fritz, who paid them heftily for the job. The two convicts are currently behind bars in Tazewell County Jail, and Adlehorn has already started a nationwide search for Fritz Feltman.'"

"Well, can you believe that?" exclaimed Christian.

"That's the man we saw in the saloon doorway the night you arrived, right?" Fredrich asked, looking at John Adlehorn's picture.

"Yes, and the other two men came with us from Chicago on The *Delta Queen*. Actually, they spent the night with us in Chicago," Christian concluded.

"Really! And you didn't know them?"

"Well, Conrad had talked with them on the *Don Quixote*, but, frankly, I didn't like the looks of either of them. You can tell a lot about a person from his eyes, and both had suspicion written not only in their eyes but also all over their faces. What's really funny, though, is that I didn't trust Marcus — well, I guess his name is John. He, too, looked suspicious, and with his unkempt beard and shabby appearance, I would never have believed that he worked for the federal officials."

"He probably dressed shabbily to fit into the crowd of common people. He must have remained 'on the job' even on the ship to America, huh?" Fredrich smiled.

"Apparently," Christian nodded.

"There's a little more to the story," Fredrich continued. "Apparently, Adlehorn has helped the Underground Railroad as well."

"What is that?" Christian asked, confusedly.

"Oh, let me try to explain. Northern parts of America have been involved with helping Black slaves escape from the South. It's a dangerous decision for men to make — smuggling Blacks. But many Northerners don't believe in slavery. The Underground Railroad is a term used for men or organizations helping Blacks escape."

Christian's thoughts returned to the night on the *Julia Belle* when the Black lady and children disappeared into the bowels of the steamboat.

"So that's what it was all about," Christian said, thinking aloud.

"What?" Fredrich questioned.

"Oh, nothing, Fredrich. Well, Conrad will never believe this story."

It made for an all-Sunday-afternoon conversation piece as the Pollmanns began to understand the concept of Underground Railroad and also realized that they would have to be careful of their character judgment in the New World. No longer in the village of Hummersen in which everyone knew his neighbor and trust was not an issue, Christian suggested that the family be wary until they understood the American way of life and could "read" people a bit better. Fredrich tried to assure them that customs were not all that much different from back home because of the large population of Germans inhabiting most of Pekin. Nevertheless, the Pollmans felt a twinge of insecurity and hesitation — despite Fredrich's encouragement — as they studied the picture once again of Nicholaas and Herman as convicted murderers and of the ragged, rough-looking John Adlehorn as a federal official working for the good of the nation.

Thirty-three

THE FIRST MONTHS IN AMERICA

Spring turned into summer and summer into autumn. It had been a rough growing season for the Midwesterners. Early summer floods had destroyed crops, and farmers were forced to replant. Fredrich and Christian as well as Conrad worked long hours into the late evening tending the fields. The harvest, however, was decent — enough to pay immediate bills and pocket a small amount of money for winter expenses. The farmers rejoiced that they had been able to survive the past harsh winter and present unpredictable summer.

An unexpected experience gave Chris the opportunity to meet the Pottawatomie chief, Shaubena. Alone in a field one fall evening just at dusk, Christian was digging potatoes when he looked up to see two Native Americans riding spotted ponies towards him. Having only seen Indians once before when aboard the *Julia Belle*, Christian wasn't sure how to react. Laying his hoe down to demonstrate his non-aggression, Chris stood still, looking into the fading sunset. Not sure if they were friendly or not, Christian waited anxiously as they dismounted. He was hoping that the older Indian was Shaubena because Christian had heard stories of the friendly Pottawatomie chief from Fredrich.

He knew that Shaubena had saved Pekin from Black Hawk who had threatened the Pottawatomies with the statement, "If the Pottawatomie nation will rise, our warriors will number as the trees of the forest."

Shaubena had replied, "If so, you will find that the white man's warriors number as the leaves on the trees of the forest."

With this daring statement and then Shaubena's continual actions to protect Pekin, Fredrich had told Chris that Black Hawk and his warriors never came within 50 miles of their river town.

The younger Indian lingered behind, carrying a blanket. Without saying a word, the older Indian pointed to the bucket of potatoes, and the brave handed Christian the blanket. With the bucket only three-quarters full, Chris was concerned that it wasn't a fair trade but agreed anyway. A handshake finalized the transaction, and the two Indians left. Christian later learned that it had, indeed, been Shaubena, who often appeared without warning to trade his goods for supplies he needed. Although stern-faced and daunting, Shaubena had always been a friend to the white people of Illinois.

School had started in September, and the Pollmann children — Mary, Elise, Jurgen, and Christoph — eagerly walked to Snell School, located at Second and Elizabeth Streets. Having learned a little English by then, they found that both German and English were spoken at school. Many children knew no English at all, and so the teacher found it necessary to interchange the languages during the lessons.

The four children would return home each day to teach new words to their siblings and parents. Each evening meal was turned into a game as the children became teachers, instructing the other youngsters and their parents in the new language.

Elizabeth and Louisa were learning English in other ways, too. They quilted once a week with other ladies of the church congregation in a vacant room above Main St. Dry Goods. The finished quilts were given to the elderly or needy families of the town. An hour a week gave the ladies a much-needed break from their endless, laborious tasks at home as well as valuable time to hear the English language spoken. The German ladies who had been in America for several years helped the newcomers learn the basic words needed to shop in the stores. Thursday mornings became a time that Elizabeth and Louisa treasured.

Autumn drifted into winter as the immigrants experienced their first new holiday — Thanksgiving. And, indeed, the Pollmanns had so much for which to be thankful — their health, families, jobs, and life in the New World. And born to Christian and Elizabeth shortly after Thanksgiving was a baby boy — Heinrich Georg. He was born on a cold Sunday morning in early December when the world was made pure and white with a sudden winter storm that dipped each tree, fence post, and chimney in a white, icy snow. With no doctor available because of the weather, Chris helped the neighbor lady, Edna, deliver the 7 pound, 2 ounce Heinrich into the world. Only a few weeks before Christmas, he was the perfect present to celebrate the blessed holiday in the New World.

Christmas Eve was a festivity beyond all celebrations. The Pollmanns had very few presents, but they had each other and most of all, love. The evening church service was held in a small store on Ann Eliza Street. Hoping to be in an actual church by Christmas, St. Johannes Church was still in temporary dwellings. As people carried candles through the snowy, star-filled night, the store was full as the congregation flowed over onto the street. Hymns sung in German could be heard up and down Ann Eliza that Christmas Eve, and except for yearning for relatives back home in Hummersen, it was a perfect, incredibly happy time for the Pollmanns.

Congregating at Fredrich and Louisa's later that evening, friends of the Pollmanns brought German food which had been prepared days in advance. Along with an evergreen, which had been cut and adorned with red ribbons and lit candles, old-world music filled the rooms as the Pollmanns celebrated the holiest of days until well after midnight.

Several days after Christmas, Christian, Elizabeth, and the children sat around the fire. It was impossible to get to school because of the snow. Another blizzard had snuck up on the Midwesterners in the middle of the night, and it continued to fall unceasingly late into the afternoon.

Jurgen was whittling and the two girls were playing with their rag dolls.

"You know, Ma, I really like it here," Margaretha said unexpectedly.

Elizabeth looked up from her sewing. Trying to hide her surprise, she nodded with a grin.

"That's good, Margaretha. I'm glad to hear you say that," remarked Elizabeth.

"Do you like it, Mama?" she asked as she moved her doll like a puppet, pretending that it was doing the talking.

Elizabeth thought how to answer. Finally, she replied, "It's not Germany, but it's getting to seem more like home."

Jurgen — who was thankful for everything and displayed this behavior each day — piped up, "I had nothing before, and now I feel like I'm living a dream — food to eat, a bed to sleep on, and lots of love from everyone. I *love* it here," he beamed.

"Lot's of love," repeated Christian. "That's the key to living, don't you think, Elizabeth?"

"Yes, I guess you're right. As long as I have all of you," she said as she hugged her children, "how can I ask for more?"

Soon it would be the new year of 1853 with a plethora of unexplored, untried adventures. The Pollmanns would suffer through untold tribulations, but they knew that the Lord would be with them throughout all of the trials as they learned to adjust to a new way of life in America. As more and more Germans joined the community from the Old World, the Pollmanns were soon the ones teaching the newcomers the language, traditions, and customs of America. They learned that on a daily basis they must attain their strength from their friends, their family, and mostly from God, which were the Old World values that Heinrich and Sophia Pollmann and Johann and Anna Haas had taught their children many years before.

Epilogue

LIFE IN AMERICA - 1852

In 1857, Christian and Fredrich Pollmann, along with a few other members, left the St. Johannes Church and formed St. Paul's German Evangelical Church. Founded on December 12, 1858, Christian and Fredrich became two of the founding fathers. While meeting in members' homes and in other churches, they purchased land for the church, school, and pastor's home. On November 6, 1859, St. Paul's German Evangelical Church was dedicated, and Pastor C. W. Lipp was secured as the first reverend.

On June 16, 1934, St. Paul's Evangelical synod united with the Reformed Church, becoming St. Paul's Evangelical and Reformed Church. Later in 1957, the Congregational Church united with St. Paul's Evangelical and Reformed Church, resulting in St. Paul's United Church of Christ. The present church, located on the corner of Eighth, Margaret, and Broadway in Pekin, was dedicated on February 15, 1953. It still possesses the doctrines and sanctions set up by the founding fathers in 1857.

Elizabeth and Christian's union produced seven children: Margaretha, Anna-Marie, Heinrich Georg, Johan, Georg B., Karl Ernst, and Georg Christian. Even though there were blessings, life was full of difficulties in the 1800s, and the death of children was the worst disaster that could befall a family. Of the seven children, all but Georg Christian — my grandfather — died either in childhood or in early adulthood.

When Elizabeth died in 1914, she had one child left — Georg. Americanizing his name, he became George Christian Pollman and married Katherine Zimmerman on November 1, 1900. Their union produced six children: Harry, Mabel Anna (my mother), Emma Marie, Minnie, George Fredrich, and Ruth Katherine. Christian died a year later at the age of 90. He had seen so much — revolution, poverty, religious persecution, and famine in Germany; in America he saw the assassination of President Lincoln, The Civil War, the coming of cars, electricity, airplanes, and the birth, life and death of many family members.

Christian had led a full life — not an easy one but one with blessings as well as heartaches. Truly, he believed in John 3:16: "For God so loved the world, that He gave his only begotten son that whosoever believeth in Him shall have eternal life." With this belief confirmed, both he and Elizabeth were buried in unmarked graves at Lakeside Cemetery, Pekin, Illinois. Their earthly lives were unimportant in comparison to their heavenly lives, and with unmarked graves, no one would be able to stand and cry where only physical remains were buried — the souls of those who believed in Christ Jesus had already risen to heavenly heights, among them Christian and Elizabeth Pollmann. However, on May 19, 2007, the first Pollman Reunion was held, and the family accumulated enough money for a beautiful tombstone to adorn the graves of Christian and Elizabeth.

Throughout his entire life, Christian had placed the Lord at the center. God was allowed to control Christian's thoughts, desires, and wishes, and when Christian Pollmann died, he knew that he would go to a far better place — his heavenly home about which he had learned in the small church in Falkenhagen, on the outskirts of the tiny village of Hummersen, Germany.

Works Cited

Avi. *The Escape from Home*. New York: 1996. Print.

Avi. *Lord Kirkle's Money*. New York: 1996. Print.

Baily, John. *The Lost German Slave Girl*. New York: 2003. Print.

"Effects of the Famine." Mar. 2007 Web. 20 Apr. 2006.

"The German 1848 Revolution: A German Perspective. Mar. 2007. Web. 17 Apr. 2006.

"In the Steerage." *Balch Online Resources*. May 2007. Web. 15 May 2006.

Jackson, Kathryn. *The Joys of Christmas*. New York: 1976. Print.

Laxton, Edward. *The Famine Ships*. New York: 1996. Print.

MacroHistory. "Reaction and Reform, 1848 to 1850." June 2007. Web. 12 May 2006.

Pekin Sesquicentennial A History 1824-1974. Print.

"Why Germans Left Home." 2007. Web. 13 Apr 2006.

Jan Frazier has been in the field of teaching for nearly forty years, first at the secondary level and currently at the university level. She has lived in Holland and still travels to Europe every year under the guise that she needs more information for her novels and creative nonfiction books, most of which have been set in Europe. She had the honor of taking high school students abroad for fifteen years and now has the privilege of taking Bradley University students to London during the January Interim. She has always believed that only so much can be taught within the four walls of the classroom, and then the students need to get into the world and "see" for themselves. Frazier has been honored with various awards for teaching as well as for her writing abilities. She has twenty books to her credit and continues to enjoy both teaching and writing.

www.ingramcontent.com/pod-product-compliance
Lightning Source LLC
Chambersburg PA
CBHW070006260626
47159CB00005B/1693